THE ALVAREZ JOURNAL

Rex Burns

A BERKLEY MEDALLION BOOK

published by

BERKLEY PUBLISHING CORPORATION

Harper and Row Publishers, Inc.
10 E. 53rd Street
New York, N.Y.

Library of Congress Catalog Card Number 75-6365

SBN 425-03347-3

BERKLEY MEDALLION BOOKS are published by
Berkley Publishing Corporation
200 Madison Avenue
New York, N.Y. 10016

BERKLEY MEDALLION BOOK ® TM 757,375

Printed in the United States of America

Berkley Medallion Edition, MARCH, 1977

to R.P. and R.C.

The following abbreviations are used in the text:

AKA	also known as
CBI	Colorado Bureau of Investigation
DALE	Office of Drug Abuse Law Enforcement; combined with the Bureau of Narcotics and Dangerous Drugs into the Drug Enforcement Agency
DEA	Drug Enforcement Agency
DPD	Denver Police Department
MEG	Metropolitan Enforcement Group
OCD	Organized Crime Division
TAD	temporary additional duty
TO	table of organization
WATS	wide area telecommunications services

1

"For you, Gabe." Suzy pressed the hold button. "Line two."

Gabriel Wager nodded to the secretary and continued filling in the form as he picked up the telephone. "Detective Wager speaking."

A familiar voice asked, "Who was that there?"

"We have a secretary now—Suzy."

"You getting mighty big time."

"She's all right. What do you have for me?" He winked at the girl, who, halfway between plain and ugly, smiled back uncertainly. Sergeant Johnston had turned down all the good-looking applicants when he smiled at them; but it was just as well—good-looking broads didn't work as hard.

"Listen, them two mamas I told you about . . ." The black voice trailed off.

"Pat and Mike?"

"Ha, yeah. I set a deal on some heroin with them."

A year ago it would have been just grass; now Denver was getting its share of hard stuff, and this new group, the Organized Crime Division, was supposed to be the answer. Like hell it would be the answer. Wager pulled a legal pad over and began taking notes. "Where and when, Fat Willy?"

"Tonight at the Landing Pad. A balloon."

Another long day. "Time?"

"Eleven-thirty."

"Inside?"

"The alley out back."

"Can you bring a friend?"

"Naw, man, it's my first score."

There was a long silence before Wager finally gave in. "I guess you'll need some bread."

1

"It's just a balloon, but it's more than I got right now."

"I wondered why you called me on the first score."

"Aw, man, us minorities got to play each other straight!"

"You're always straighter when you're broke, Willy." And up yours with that soul-brother crap.

"Ha, ain't that the truth."

"I'll meet you at the Frontier about"—he checked his watch —"six o'clock."

"Right, man."

He hung up and turned back to the preliminary he was working on: Robbins, Roland—aka Spider. Type of request, grounds for suspicion, qualifications of informants and their depositions, exchange of information with other agencies, results of preliminary investigation. He was on that last part now, checking the key dates against the contact cards and case journal.

"It's for you again, Gabe."

"Jesus Christ!" He punched the lit button. "Detective Wager speaking."

"Johnston here. Did you get the word Simpson's quitting?"

The sergeant's office was ten feet away. If it was good news, he walked to Wager's desk; if it was bad, he phoned. "No shit! What for?"

"He got that sergeant's job in Littleton."

Wager gazed at the stack of pending cases on his desk. "When do we get his replacement?"

"We just got Denby."

"That was for Billington!" And they had to wait three months for that one.

"I know that, Gabe, but the Inspector told me not to count on any new personnel this fiscal year."

Wager's voice gained the Spanish accent that came when he was angry: "I hope he's not counting on many busts this fiscal year."

"We're doing what we can, Gabe."

"Yeah." He hung up and gazed out the window at the distant mountains, hazy and dry through the city's heat and smog. Damn Simpson and damn Littleton for hiring him away. He'd almost damn Billington for going, too, except he knew how much his ex-partner had worried over the deci-

2

sion. And how much it had cost him to urge Billy to take the better job. Nobody in his right mind turned down a federal job, and Billy deserved the break. He was a good cop, a good man; he had a family and needed the pay. Still, Wager and Billy had been partners, had come as a team from the Crimes Against Persons Division when Johnston set up the Special Narcotics Section of the OCD. Now Wager was still here and Billy had moved on. And now Simpson. Crap.

"Where's Detective Denby, Suzy?"

"He's still going through orientation. I think he's supposed to be in district court now."

"Thanks." He finally finished the Robbins preliminary, penciled *"Ed—please rush"* across the blue cover, and handed it to Suzy. Then he filled out a contact card on Willy's tip and thumbed through the files for Pat and Mike: Browne, Labelle Carol; and Halsam, Ann Louise—aka Osborne. No file on Halsam (Osborne); he'd have to survey the central files in the Denver Police Department. Browne had a thin folder: "Negro female, b. 10 Nov. 1941, 5'4", prostitution arrest 1969, probation, no violations, rumored drug dealing 1971 +." "Suzy—" He stopped at the look on her face. "What's the matter?"

"I was just leaving. It's after five."

"Well, why aren't you leaving, for God's sake? It's after five!"

She giggled, and said unconvincingly, "I can stay if you want."

"It's not that important." And sure as hell not worth the hassle that would come from asking a union member for ten minutes' overtime. "First thing tomorrow, see what DPD has on these names." He waved the file.

"Yes, sir."

She was gone through the warren of small offices that cluttered the second floor of the old building. Wager listened for a moment to the heavy, almost airless pause of the waiting desks and typewriters, the silence of radio transmitters turned off against the constant tally of reports and queries, the distant music of a portable radio helping the duty watch pass the time. Add the smell of a little shoe polish and aftershave lotion, and it would be like a squad bay on a Sunday afternoon, the way he used to like them: no bustling pressures of

3

people and only the quiet of the guard detail going its appointed rounds. A long time ago. He'd be at least a gunnery sergeant now if he'd stayed in. Or dead. You didn't get quick promotions without a few deaths. Still, no regrets; he had lousy pay, an insecure job, and hours longer than a whore's Saturday night, but it was his own time and that made all the difference.

He relocked the file drawer and scribbled a note to remind Suzy: "Any DPD number on Halsam, Ann; and recent arrests on Browne, Labelle Carol," and anchored it under the roller of her typewriter. Five-fifteen; forty-five minutes to get to the Frontier and see Willy. Keying the GE radiopack on his belt, he called Denby and waited. Two clicks answered, and a few minutes later the new man's voice came through: "This is two-one-four. I was in the courtroom and couldn't talk."

"Two-one-two. Can you meet me at the Frontier at six?"

A pause. "I better call home. My wife usually holds supper for me."

"Ten-four." Wager slid the antenna into the radio and holstered it, frowning at Denby's hesitation but glad that he made the right choice. Time for one more item from the pending pile—an envelope opened, retaped, his name scrawled over the original address in Sergeant Johnston's handwriting: "Gabe, check it out." Gabe, Simpson's quitting. Gabe, we don't have a replacement. Crapcrap.

The letter was from the Seattle office of the Drug Enforcement Agency, stating that one Eddie Hart—busted in Seattle by DEA agents—named the Rare Things Import Shop, 1543 West Thirty-eighth Street, Denver, Colorado, as a front for smuggling marijuana into the United States at the rate of five hundred to a thousand pounds a week.

Staring out the window, Wager tried to recall the name of the import shop's owner, but there was no response, no little quiver of memory. Nothing that clustered a dozen other facts into something like a pattern that could be corroborated and gradually built into a case. And it was odd that the tip came in this fashion: usually such information came by telephone instead of mail. Either the DEA was stingier than the Denver Police Department or the transmitting agent didn't think much of the lead. Which was all right. There was always too much unsubstantiated information anyway: anonymous phone calls, a fellow detective's vague hunch, an unexplained contact, revenge tips, notes from distant agencies. Anything to do with narcotics was channeled onto Sergeant Ed Johnston's desk and unfailingly he assigned them—one, two, sometimes three at a time—to the detectives. If they rang a bell, they were priority. If not, you got to them when you could. Wager stuck another note on Suzy's typewriter: "See if licensing has anything on this business address," and jotted down the Thirty-eighth Street number. Then he headed for the Frontier Lounge.

In the late-afternoon heat, the Frontier Lounge was a hole of cool blackness smelling of stale beer and rustling with the tired but comfortable talk of a few hours after quitting time. Wager blinked away the purple sun blindness and, as his eyes began to pick out shapes against the shaded lights, groped through the scattered tables toward the row of booths. A curl of cigarette smoke rose over a high seat back and Wager glanced in. "Hello, Fat Willy."

The black's big round face, darker in the shadow of his wide-brimmed hat, peeked rapidly past Wager, then grinned welcome. "You hot for this—what you call them?—Pat and Mike?"

"We've been hearing about them off and on. How'd you get on to it?"

A shrug. "Aw, you know, man; just around."

Wager nodded and signaled Rosy, the waitress. "What'll you have, Willy?"

"Vodka and Seven." Willy waited until Rosy had their orders and was gone. "They claim they can get as much stuff as I want."

"What's their source?"

"Come on, man!" Fat Willy threw back his head and laughed, teeth a white flash against his sweat-glinting face.

"If you knew, you'd tell me, wouldn't you, Willy?"

"Aw, yeah!"

"Tell me this, then: have you ever heard of Eddie Hart?"

"Hart?" He flipped through his mental card-file of names, then shook his head. "No, what's his act?"

"How about the Rare Things Import Shop?"

This time, Fat Willy's answer came almost too quickly:

"Naw, but if you feed my need, maybe, baby, I can dig a lead—ha!"

"I'm interested."

"And I heed!"

The drinks came and with them Denby, medium height, hair fashionably long and dry, moving awkwardly as he groped in the dimness and peered into one booth after another.

"Here we are."

"Jesus, I can't see a thing." Denby scrubbed his nose with a handkerchief.

"Hey, Wager, what's going on?"

"Take it easy, Willy. This is Detective Denby—he's just joined the division. I want to get him started with Pat and Mike."

"Man, you didn't tell me nothing about this dude. I don't dig this surprise shit!"

Wager forced patience into his voice. "Pat and Mike don't know Officer Denby. I helped bust one of them on a prostitution charge six years ago. If she recognizes me, your ass is peanut butter." He smoothed out five twenty-dollar bills and slid them across the table. "Here's for the balloon and a little extra."

Willy stared at the money and then at Denby and Wager; then he quickly folded it between his thick fingers and poked it into a coat pocket. "Well, I reckon it's all right. What's your name? Dumpy?"

"Denby. Phil Denby."

"Bring him in on your third or fourth score," said Wager. "We'll handle it from there."

Willy drained his glass. "Let's make it the fourth one."

"OK."

The black slid heavily across the wooden seat and nodded at Denby. "Pleased to meet you."

"Pleased to meet you."

"I'll call *you* next week, Wager."

"Fine."

They watched the wide figure, draped in its white linen suit, disappear toward the door.

"He wasn't pleased to meet me."

6

"Don't get strung out over it. Did you see how fast the son of a bitch picked up that money? He'll get over his mad when he needs more."

"What's this Pat and Mike thing?"

Wager ordered two more beers from Rosy and, feeling out the younger detective's reactions, sketched what he knew of the lesbians' dealing.

"And I'm to be Willy's friend at the fourth meet?"

"Right. You make some buys on your own and then bring in another friend later on. When they get set up, your friend will run the buy and bust, and Willy keeps his cover. They'll think you're the snitch."

"Willy gets a lot of free dope out of this."

"It's his to keep if he doesn't get caught."

"It sure as hell seems funny to support his habit with tax money."

"Dinero llama dinero."

"What?"

"Old Spanish saying. It takes money to make money."

"That's an old Spanish saying?"

"Rough translation."

"Oh."

They finished their beer and Wager asked the younger man if he wanted to cover Willy's meet tonight. Denby nodded glumly. "But I got to drop by home first. Helen was pissed off when I called. She had plans or something."

"She better get used to it. You'll be juggling maybe a dozen cases, and when a break comes, you can't leave it for the day shift. We don't *have* a day shift."

"I know, Gabe. No complaints about joining up. It's just that Helen . . . Well, never mind."

He did not have to finish. Wager had seen too many policemen married to women who weren't really policemen's wives. Himself among them. A real cop found the right woman or did without. "I'll see you at the office lot around ten. And you better get some gum."

"Gum?"

"You don't want to go home smelling of beer."

"Amen!"

The Landing Pad's neon sign winked pink rotor blades over the door. Wager drove past slowly, checking the license plates and the cars nosed into the curb; silent beside him, Denby's head swiveled restlessly. Usually, each detective would be alone in his car, linked by the radiopacks to half a dozen channels. Wager liked it better that way since Billy left. But Denby was new and it was wise to stay close to him. Wise until he knew more about the new man.

"There's a couple of out-of-state plates. Louisiana."

Nodding, Wager turned the corner and in to the alley; New Orleans was a major port of entry for heroin; hell, the whole Gulf Coast was open. Or they could be tourists looking for the gay life. He cruised past the lighted back door with its stack of dented garbage cans, looked for an empty lot to slide the car in, and found a narrow driveway between sagging fences; he backed in and turned off the motor. In the silence, the radio's constant traffic was loud with reports of District 2 pursuits, requests, notices. He reached beneath the seat for the power pack and turned down the volume.

"You ever hear of the Rare Things Import Shop?"

"Me? Naw. Where's it at?"

"Fifteen forty-three West Thirty-eighth Street."

"No. I must have been by it, but I don't remember it." Denby blew his nose savagely into a red handkerchief. "Something in bloom."

"Why don't you get a prescription?"

"I don't like pills."

It figured. Since Denby had joined the unit, Wager had begun to think twice before taking even an aspirin. Maybe the health-food cult had something going for it.

"I was reading where even coffee was supposed to give you a heart attack," Denby said.

Wager thought of the gallons of coffee that went through him each day. "Maybe I better switch to tea."

"Some English doctor says tea makes birth defects—some kind of nervous disorder, he says. Helen told me about it."

"Christ, it's safer to starve to death."

They lapsed into one of those long silences that are so much a part of surveillance. Finally, the younger man asked, "What's in bloom?"

8

"Ragweed."

He blew again. "Wouldn't you know it. We just got rid of the Russian thistle in the back yard and now it's ragweed."

Another silence while they waited and stared at the closed back door of the Landing Pad, with its single bulb glowing on the scarred paint. Denby looked at his watch. "Quarter past. You think Willy was putting us on?"

"No. He's pretty legitimate."

Denby thought a few moments. "Then why are we here?"

"You never can tell. Besides, I want you to see the suspects."

"If we bust Pat and Mike, do you think one of them will turn informer?"

"Be worth a try. Female Concerned Individuals are hard to get."

"Yeah. I'd like to start building up a stable of CIs."

There was only one way to do it: be on call twenty-four hours a day. "They come and they go."

"Yeah."

They listened to the muted radio naming the district's action. Denby checked his watch again. "I wish that bastard would hurry up."

Wager nodded and waited. Then, from the other end of the alley and walking slowly into the light of the doorway with a familiar roll of the shoulders, Fat Willy strolled past without pausing. Wager and Denby slid down in the car seat and watched the linen shadow. He walked toward them, stared hard at their car parked in the black of the narrow driveway, and disappeared around the corner.

"Did he see us?"

"I don't know. He's checking things out."

A few moments later, a dog barked behind them and the sound of slow footsteps came up to the car. Willy's face, a wide shadow beneath the hat, peered in the window. "My, oh my, the fuzz."

Wager tried to sound happier than he felt. "Hello, Willy."

"You going to bust them tonight? You want to blow my cover?"

"I want Officer Denby to get a look at them."

"Mmm." The hat brim wagged slowly from side to side.

9

"Sometimes I believe you don't trust me, brother."

"Sometimes you're right, Willy. But we're the best each other's got."

A muffled gurgle of laughter. "I sure ain't getting no bargain! Catch your act next time."

The gray shape sauntered back toward the lighted door.

"He's a cocky son of a bitch, ain't he! You think Pat and Mike spotted us, too?"

"We'll find out." Wager watched as Willy lit a cigarette and flipped the glowing match into the dark. It bounced once on the tar and died out. A few minutes later, the hat brim lifted and Willy stared toward the corner of the bar and nodded. A thin Negro woman in Levis and halter stepped into the light.

"That's Labelle Browne." She was older and had changed her hair, but Wager still recognized her.

She held something out in one hand and opened the other for the money; Willy shook his head and stuck his fingertip into the balloon and tasted it, then handed her the cash. She counted it quickly and left. Willy faded into the darkness.

"Just like that." Denby clicked his tongue in disgust. "We should have popped the bitch right then."

Wager shrugged. "What's the rush? Let's build a case on her first. Hold it!" A second dim figure trotted down the alley in front of the dark car and crossed the patch of light like a frightened cat: same Levis and halter, but shorter and with hair teased out in a wide Afro.

"I'll bet that's Halsam, and I'll bet she was set out somewhere to cover the deal."

"Goddam! You think she's got a weapon?"

"You know it."

Denby's wide eyes caught the light. "She'd use it, too!"

"She looked scared enough to. But I think they're more afraid of a rip-off than a bust."

"I'm glad we didn't move in!"

"Now we'll know what to look for when we do." Ringing loud though his memory was the sound of the first shot fired at him, and the cold, sick feeling of fear and hate that still came with that memory. Fear, hate, suspicion—it was a great life if it didn't kill you first. But if you can't do the time, don't do the crime—old jailhouse philosophy—and most of these

10

people could do the time. They had proved it. The cop better prove it, too.

They sat another ten minutes or so; then Wager, with lights off, pulled the car down the alley and swung onto the street. He turned on the headlights for one last pass in front of the bar.

"Tomorrow why don't you check vehicle registration for the kind of car Pat and Mike drive?"

"OK." Denby blew his nose again and looked at his watch. "Jesus—after midnight. Helen wanted to go to a movie tonight."

"Too bad."

"Business is business, I guess."

"Yeah."

He let Denby out at the office parking lot and watched the new Fury III slide under the gleam of empty streetlights. Denby had a wife and a new kid, a house, and probably a cat or dog. Family. Liked to take his wife to the movies. Deep down, liked to have her tell him what to do. Wager didn't think Denby would last long in the narcotics division.

2

Wager reached the aging office building across from the capitol at nine and climbed the dim narrow stairs to the OCD headquarters. On the second-floor landing, in her box of sterile space, Mrs. Gutierrez smiled through the bulletproof plexiglass and pressed the "open" buzzer to unlock the inner door. Mrs. Gutierrez and her little window were unit security; the few times Wager had seen anyone held up for clearance, she seemed terribly embarrassed and terribly pleased when the person was finally admitted. As usual, she was terribly happy to see him this morning. Wager couldn't stand people who were terribly anything.

He twisted between desks and thin partitions that bounced back the rattle of typewriters and conversations, to the relative quiet of the narcotics unit's corner. Suzy was out for the moment, but anchored to his desk by the clean ashtray was a note: "DPD file on Browne, Labelle, in top drawer. Nothing on Halsam (Osborne), Ann. Owner of Rare Things Import S.: Montoya, Eduardo Guillermo, 655 W. 8th Ave., Denver. No DPD file on that person."

He rolled the name through his mind and again sought an echo; still nothing, still no tingle of recognition or "aha" of something clicking into place. Except . . . Spanish name—imports—a natural setup for a Mexican connection. Maybe something there: check it out. Good title for a detective story: "Wager Checks It Out."

The secretary came back with a pot of fresh coffee and a cheery "Good morning, Gabe!"

Wager did not like cheery good mornings, either. "Does Ed have any answer on the Robbins preliminary yet?"

"The Inspector said he wanted to see you and Detective Denby on that."

Scalding hot coffee for a heart attack, and a fight with the Inspector for high blood pressure. "What for?"

"I don't know, but he didn't sound upset."

Then he could wait. Wager turned to work on routine papers: sheaves of forms that seemed to peak in quarterly, semiannual, and annual waves, always the same in content and result. Someone somewhere must have one hell of a big pile of worthless paper, because none of it ever changed anything. It was ten o'clock before he looked up again and saw Denby sit on the edge of his desk. The baggy redness of the younger man's eyes made Wager rub at his own. "Didn't you get any sleep last night?"

From behind his handkerchief, Denby mumbled, "Allergies—the wind's up today and it's really bad. And Helen wanted to talk half the night."

Wager thought he should learn how to shut her up. He pushed his copy of the Robbins file at Denby. "Look this over. I've asked Ed to let you handle the action on it."

The younger detective managed a smile. "Good news! I was beginning to feel like a fifth wheel." He lost himself in the folder.

Wager asked Suzy to find out when the Inspector would be free, then burrowed again into the data that would contribute to the unit sergeant's report, which would contribute to the Inspector's report, which would contribute to the division report, which would contribute to the DA's report, which would contribute . . . Suzy interrupted his thoughts: "He can see you now."

It was the kind of tiny, tidy office that you did not bring your coffee cup into. Sonnenberg nodded to two wooden captain's chairs jammed against the wall and, talking into the telephone, gestured at Wager to close the door. He finished and turned to the blue-covered preliminary on Robbins. "Where does this one get his merchandise, Gabe?"

"We haven't been able to find out, sir. He's been under surveillance by DEA since, I think, August '72. But no one's spotted his supplier."

"I'd like to get something more than another bagman. We're getting a hell of a lot more heroin in from somewhere."

"Yes, sir."

14

"Will Robbins work with us if we hang something on him?"

"He might."

"You don't sound too sure."

"No, sir. Other people have tried, but he wanted nothing to do with it."

"See what you can do anyway. Come down on him hard and see what you can do."

"Yes, sir." What the hell else did Sonnenberg think he was going to do?

The Inspector tapped a pencil on the blue cover. "Are you handling this?"

"I was. Detective Denby has it now." The cover letter said that, and Wager knew Sonnenberg had read it.

The Inspector's eyes, chips of pale blue, studied the younger detective. "You've had experience in this?"

"Yes, sir. I wore a uniform for four years, and was on burglary for two more."

"Hmm."

"Detective Denby's very capable, Inspector." He damned well better be.

"I'm sure he is. What are you on now, Gabe?"

"Quarterly reports and CI calls. And looking into that tip from Seattle."

"And Ashcroft is still tied up in court?"

"Yes, sir." Which Sonnenberg also knew.

The Inspector tapped again until the silence grew embarrassing and Wager finally said what he knew Sonnenberg wanted: "When we're set to bust Robbins, I'll go along with Detective Denby if you want me to."

"I wish you would." The icy eyes turned toward Denby. "You've got a good record or you wouldn't be here. But it's my policy to have a man well-grounded in our procedures before he's left on his own. If Detective Wager gave you the case, that's a mark in your favor, and I'll leave you on it. But I want Wager to observe your first few operations and report your progress to me. And I want you to learn from Wager. Any questions?"

"No, sir."

The Inspector turned back to Wager. "What about the Seattle thing?"

Glad for a different topic, Wager told the little he knew.

"I'd rather go after the heroin than the marijuana," the Inspector said.

"Yes, sir. But this could be a lot of grass."

"I suppose it's worth a little time, but don't overdo it." He turned back to the blue file and tapped Robbins' name again. "I'll have a DEA man work with you on this. Billington's still over there, isn't he?"

"Yes, sir."

"Well, nail Robbins good and maybe we can turn him into a CI."

Back in their office, Denby sat glumly on the edge of the desk. "What's so hard about busting a two-bit pusher?"

"Don't let it eat you. Sonnenberg's up tight because we're a new unit and appropriations time's coming up. If the unit doesn't prove out"—Wager shrugged—"we go back to burglary."

"I should've opted for homicide."

Wager poured fresh coffee into the cold pool in his cup. "Organized crime's here to stay, and dope's a part of it. We'll always have a job. Hell, we got more than we can handle now."

"My wife wanted me to be a fireman."

"Is she trying to get rid of you?"

"She thought it would be more romantic." Denby sneezed and dabbed at his eyes.

Suzy said "Just a moment" into the phone and aimed it at Wager. "It's Agent Billington from DEA. He wants to know about Robbins."

"Take it, Denby. Set it up." He tried to avoid talking to Billy since the transfer.

"For when? When do you want it?"

"Let's try tonight—the informant said he's hot all week."

The younger man hopped for the phone. "This is Detective Denby. No, he'll be with us, but I'm handling it from this end. How about tonight—the CI said he'd be hot all week. Fine. Why don't we meet about eleven?" He glanced inquiringly at Wager, who nodded. "Right, we have the warrant. Right. That's what our informant said. Fine." Denby hung up. He looked embarrassed. "He—ah—preferred you, I think."

"We've worked together before. Billy's a good man."

16

Wager slid another form under his pen and began filling in the blanks.

"Does he try to rub it all over you that he's a federal officer?"

"No. He used to be in this office."

"Oh."

"Here—you might as well learn the really important part of this job. See these interagency request forms?" He showed Denby how to fill in the rough for Suzy to type later. Then he worked through lunch into the afternoon while Denby rounded up the Robbins warrant and the various agencies involved in the night's move. At four, Simpson came by to check in his keys and equipment and say good-bye to Wager.

"Say, we'll still be seeing a lot of each other." The tall, stoop-shouldered man gripped Wager's brown hand in both of his. Denby said a brief "Pleased to meet you" and moved back to his desk. It was an awkward moment for Wager: a sense of being left behind, a feeling of betrayal, a desire not to show any ill temper. It was Simpson's choice, and, like everybody else, he had the right to move.

"You'll do a good job out there. It'll be nice to have a good man out there."

"Well, I don't know; I'll give it a try anyhow. Say, when you're in the area, come by for a cup of coffee."

"Right. And you know where we are."

"Right."

Simpson was gone and Wager sat staring wearily out the window. A sergeant's rating, regular hours, civil service security—he couldn't blame Simpson for taking the better job. Still, you always measured yourself against your co-workers, and Wager knew who the better man was. And he also knew he would have turned down the job if he had been asked—Simpson was a family man and he wasn't. But he hadn't even been asked. He would have liked to have been asked.

Denby cleared his throat. "I've got a four-man team: you and me, a man from Metro Enforcement Group—Masters—and Billington, the DEA man. You know Masters?"

"A tall black, heavyset, late twenties?"

"I only talked to him on the phone. He sounded tough."

"He is. He's a good one to have along."

"You think that's enough people?"

"I think that's all the outside help Johnston wants to pay for, and we don't have any more inside."

"Do you think it's too many? There's no sense getting Johnston pissed off."

"I think it's just fine."

Denby nodded and leafed through the Xeroxed sheets of the Robbins file one more time. Finally he looked up. "There's already enough here for a conspiracy charge."

"Conspiracy's not worth a fart in a jury trial. We need a possession charge. Any idiot civilian can understand possession: there's the man, there's the dope, there's where they were together. Unless some assistant DA can't even handle that."

"You think the CI's right about tonight?"

"He said he'd call if he heard different."

"I guess if he's wrong there's always another night."

"Always."

"It's set for the Melody Lounge. You want to meet here and go with me?"

"Where are you meeting the others?"

"On the corner of Colfax and Race. We didn't want too many cars in the area."

"I'll see you there."

"OK." He leafed through the file again, reluctant to put it down, feeling—Wager knew—his hand already reaching for Robbins' neck and the excitement that went with that reach.

"Goddam—six two, a hundred and forty pounds! Skinny son of a bitch, ain't he?"

"He's known to carry a weapon."

They both thought of the small headline on page 3 of the morning paper: "BOULDER POLICEMAN KILLED."

"Who doesn't, these days," Denby said.

Wager nodded.

There was a long pause, which Denby broke. "What about the Seattle tip?"

"I'll go by tomorrow and eyeball the place."

"Couldn't we get a search warrant based on the agent's information?"

"I'd like to do a little groundwork first."

"What about a phone tap?"

Wager was surprised at Denby's ignorance. "Not a chance
18

without some corroborating evidence to show a crime in progress at said location." It was going to be a long break-in period.

Denby blew his nose again as his eyes slid away from Wager's.

"What's the matter?"

"Nothing . . ."

"Come on, Denby. What's the problem?"

The handkerchief flapped. "I don't know. It just seems— well, chickenshit! I mean, if you know this place is suspect, why not just walk in there with a no-knock and surprise the bastards before they can get rid of the evidence!"

"And squeeze them until they break."

"Yeah!"

Pouring another cup of coffee, Wager shook his head. "You sound like a DALE agent. Do you know our unit doesn't *have* an automatic weapon?" He tapped the plated .45 magnum on his belt. "Only these little cannons."

Denby blinked. "What's that mean?"

"It means that we build cases for court. We don't just go out and start chopping people up unless we're absolutely legitimate."

"Where there's smoke, there's fire."

"It doesn't make any difference what *we* think. We've got to build a case for the court—one a fumble-brained idiot could win. Our feelings don't convict anybody; it's the jury's feelings that count. And it's hard enough to get warrants when we have the court's confidence. Don't blow that confidence by running out and busting everybody who feels wrong to you."

"Well, it seems to me"—he groped for the word—"too cautious, I guess."

Wager spoke with his heaviest accent: "Do you mean cowardly, my friend?"

"Naw. I didn't mean that. Hell, everybody knows better than that. I just think an officer should spend more time charging and less time sitting on his ass with paperwork. If an officer doesn't move fast, he doesn't step on cockroaches."

"You listen good: there's such a thing as moving too fast, such a thing as blowing a case from insufficient evidence or illegal evidence, and in the narc game it's awful easy to do. By the sweet toes of little Lord Jesus, if you ever do it to me,

I'll nail you to the wall. Is that clear? Is it?''

"It's clear.''

He heard his own breathing loud against Denby's sullen silence, and the quickness of his anger made him feel almost guilty. Denby was young and would be hard-charging if his wife let him; he had a number of convictions on the burglary squad and that showed skill. It would be worse to make him overcautious; there were already enough timeservers who had been ground into inaction by the growing restrictions on police procedure. And, above all, Wager was the first to admit that he didn't know everything about this job. He was just another detective in a second-rate city with a police department to match, and there were a lot of people a lot of places who knew the business better than he did. It was smart to remember that; not that remembering it made Denby any better, but it gave Wager more patience.

"Here''—he held out his hand—"let me get you a refill.''

Denby hesitated a moment; then he shoved the cup across the desk. "Thanks.''

"Sugar and cream?''

"Black.''

"I have to cut mine with sugar and cream. It's a lot of coffee by the end of the day.''

"I know what you mean.''

They sipped in silence for a couple of minutes; then Denby asked, "You sure you want me to handle the Robbins thing?''

"I'm sure.''

"Thanks.'' He finished his cup of coffee. "See you about quarter till.''

"We'll nail him.''

The day's wind had brought one of the late-summer thunderstorms that boil out of the mountains and across the South Platte valley around quitting time. Wager, eating supper at a diner, in one of his favorite booths by the window, watched the secretaries and office help scatter into honking cars and buses that splashed through the suddenly filled gutters and hail-rattled streets. By the time he finished, the rain had stopped and the streets were draining; here and there, pebbled in the streaks of neon light, patches of asphalt rose through the sheets of water. Later, after a nap, when he parked and walked to meet Denby, the air still smelled of wet

20

freshness, but even in the steely glare of the streetlights he could see the concrete already dry and beginning to collect its new layer of dust.

He spotted Denby by the door of a small camera shop and shook hands with Masters and Billington. Billy looked the same, but both he and Wager felt the distance between them now and they fumbled through the greeting.

"Is he in there?"

The black agent nodded. "I just went through. He's at a table in the back next to the toilet."

"Back door?"

"Locked from the outside, but it can be opened from inside—one of them pushbars."

"He'll have to be taken from the front?"

"Worse than that. There's a pool table a little over halfway. A lot of light for anybody coming at him."

Denby looked at Wager; the younger man's excitement was more intense now, but it was quiet. That was a good sign. "What do you think?"

"It's what we came for. How about you?"

Billington shrugged, lank blond hair dropping raggedly over his collar. "Want me to go in with Masters?"

"It's Denby's show. I'm just along for the ride."

"I'll go in with Masters," Denby said. "Why don't you two cover the back?"

"Give us five."

There was another awkward moment of unfamiliar politeness as Billington asked Wager what position he wanted and Wager left it up to Billy to choose first. The agent took the short leg of the alley, Wager the recessed doorway directly across from the back of the lounge. From there, he could head off the suspect if he turned away from Billington, but he would still be out of Billy's line of fire.

Wager checked his watch—about two minutes to go. Breathing deep and slow, he crouched against the cool door and waited. In the distance, near the old train depot, an emergency vehicle pumped its hollow wail; in front of the lounge, traffic rushed past with the slap of tires and occasional rapping pipes. Wager's radio clicked and Denby's tense voice came over: "You set, two-one-two?"

"Roger."

A second later, Billington's laconic "Me, too."

"OK—we're going in."

They waited in a gloom made darker by the street glare shining over the low buildings. Billington was invisible, but Wager could sense him there and it felt good—less alone, less vulnerable. He couldn't remember what it was like before Billy joined up with him, but it couldn't have been any worse than just after the transfer when he had to keep reminding himself that Billy wouldn't be at the other end of the radiopack or just around the corner keeping Wager's back clean. They had been a good team.

The two men waited. No sound, no noise, none of the half-expected muffled pops of short-barreled weapons. Silence. Then Wager's radio clicked and a voice that was only something like Denby's hooted, "He sees us—he's spotted us—he's running for the toilet—he's going for the toilet."

"Ten-four." But no answer; in his excitement Denby was pressing the transmit button, and his voice—distant from the speaker—came through: "Get the fuck out of the way!" Then Wager heard the crackle of old paint as a sealed window was pried open and the long dark shadow of a leg hung against the building's side. Then both legs were gliding down. Wager held back until he saw the figure stretched out, toes just above the alley and both hands still gripping the windowsill, before shouting, "Police officers! Don't move, you're covered!"

The figure dropped to the ground and froze against the wall, hands still high, as Wager's hammer clicked loud in the alley.

"You got me, you got me—don't shoot! I ain't armed, don't shoot!"

"Billy!" It was the familiar automatic shout, and all the embarrassment was gone. Wager sprinted to the figure and kicked the man's heels apart, then ran a hand over his thin body and twisted his arms behind for the handcuffs.

Billington clicked them on and called up to the face peering out the open window, "OK out here."

"Right. Search the son of a bitch good. He flushed something down the toilet."

Wager read the suspect his rights as he started going

22

through pockets. Nothing. No baggies, no capsules, no balloons, nothing.

"What'd you do, Robbins, swallow it?"

"What, man? The only thing I got to swallow's this shit you're handing me."

Denby and Masters ran around the corner of the alley and came panting up to the group. "Anything?" Denby asked.

"Nothing. Serve him anyway. We'll vacuum his pockets."

"Jesus God! Man, what you people hassling me for?"

Denby stuffed a paper in the vest pocket of the man's plaid coat. "Warrant for the arrest of Roland Robbins. You read him his rights?"

"Done." Wager turned him around. "Let's get him in." The excitement of the bust ebbed fast, leaving the disgusted, incomplete feeling of no evidence. And the night was just beginning.

"Hey, brother, what you doing with these ofay pigs? What you doing, now?"

Masters' large shadow leaned over the thin black. "Don't brother me, you motherfuck. I'm gonna see you get burned hot!"

"Shee-it!"

Masters bounced the handcuffed figure against the wall with a soft thud. "You pushed to my nephew and he OD'ed, man, and I'm gonna burn your black ass."

"Hey, man, that ain't my fault!"

"Shee-it!" Masters' knee pumped into the suspect's crotch and sent him, gasping and doubled, down the wall.

"Hold it, Charlie, hold it now!"

From the ground, eyes luminous with hate, Robbins grunted, "Yeah, niggershit, hold it. You ain't got nothing on me, you son of a bitch."

Masters dragged Robbins up by the coat front, lapel threads ripping. "I don't need anything *on* you, boy, because I *got* you," he said.

Robbins' face twisted in anger and his hot eyes said what his mouth wouldn't.

Waiting, Masters held him; Robbins hung silent and tense. Finally, Masters said, "Let's drag this shit downtown."

* * *

23

Wager held his tired sigh until he was out of Robbins' sight; then he poured himself another cup of now tasteless coffee, and cracked the stiff vertebrae in his back. Two-thirty. The interrogation rooms were quiet this early in the morning; here and there a fluorescent glare still burned white, but the only action was across the room at table 3, where Robbins sat sullen and defiant as Masters and Denby stared at him.

"Look, Robbins," Masters said, "if we had enough for a warrant, we've got enough for a case against you."

"Where's my free lawyer?"

"Look, I'm giving you a chance. We might work something out if you give us a little information."

Silence.

"Let's send the son of a bitch up to Cañon City, Denby. He'd be screaming in a week."

"I been busted before and never finked."

"This way you've got a chance, Robbins. The other way"—Denby shook his head sadly—"nothing. You're sure to get burned."

"Where's my free lawyer? A honky one. I don't want none of that Chicano shit."

Wager walked into the hall and sank onto a waiting bench. Robbins would not give in, he knew. Not this time. Maybe the next time. Or the time after that. Or the next one. But not this time. There wasn't enough on him. Wager leaned against the plaster wall and rubbed his burning eyes. Billy had gone home quickly after making a card for his day section, telling Wager it was good to work with him again. And, Wager admitted to himself, it was; they had been a good team. But it was funny: now that he'd worked with Billy, he didn't miss the team any more. Funny.

He yawned and wished he could go home, too, but Denby was still wound up trying to get Robbins to turn. It was a waste of time; better to book him and let the lab see if there were enough traces for possession. Better to go home and sleep so tomorrow's calls could be handled. He sipped at the styrofoam cup and tried to keep his mind blank so time would pass unnoticed. It was that stage of the morning when he was depressed by the odor of old coffee and a weary night, depressed to think how minutes that seemed so slow now were forever gone. And for what? For nothing. *Así corriendo la vida:* in haste even with slow steps.

The voices stopped, and there was a silence; after a while Wager heard the chairs scraping. It was over; Robbins had held out. In a few moments, the thin Negro in handcuffs was led to the lockup section by a uniform officer. Wager stood up from the bench and stretched. "We'll see him again," he said to Masters and Denby.

"*I* sure as hell will," Masters said. "Good night, Gabe."

"Good night, Charlie."

He walked Denby to their cars in the compound.

"That son of a bitch will be out tomorrow. You think we should work on him again in the morning?"

Wager yawned and shook his head. "I think we should get some sleep."

"The Inspector's going to be really pissed that we didn't get him with the dope."

He would be, Wager knew; but to hell with Sonnenberg. It had been a fair fight and they'd lost, and that was all there was to it. Especially at three in the morning. "He knows the way things go. I'll see you tomorrow."

"Yeah. Jesus Christ, what a grind."

For politeness' sake, they stood a few moments in the cold morning air and talked about the grind. Then Denby climbed into his blue Fury III and glided into the empty street. Wager, almost awake now that he was out of the stuffy air of the police building, turned to the district channel and listened to police calls as he drove slowly to his empty apartment.

3

The note from the sergeant's desk told him to report as soon as he came in; and while Wager was completing the journal on Robbins, he looked up to see Johnston coming toward him. He must have been waiting.

"Morning, Gabe. What happened last night?"

"He got rid of it before we could grab him."

"Sonnenberg's upset about it."

"I figured. It couldn't be helped."

"Did Denby do all right?"

"He handled it as well as could be expected—followed procedures, carried it out with no injuries to the officers involved or to the suspect. Robbins just got rid of the evidence; you know how it is."

The sergeant frowned and lit a cigarette, offering one to Wager, who refused as usual. "I know. But the Inspector, ah, has some worries about him. You know, new man and all. He really wanted you to handle it so there'd be no screw-ups. He thought Robbins might turn informer if he was busted solid enough."

"You saw Denby's record."

"Sure, sure. He looks good on paper. Don't we all. But Sonnenberg wanted Robbins bad. He doesn't want this division to turn into another Metro unit and neither do I."

Too many departments used the metropolitan task forces as a chance to get rid of poor personnel; hell, what district chief wanted to give away good men? "Me either, Ed. That's the reason I haven't taken leave since I've been here—so we'll have time to screen people before accepting them." And because too goddamned many of them transferred out!

"I know, Gabe; we all feel the same way."

"Denby's an experienced officer, and that bust last night

27

was nothing new for him. He handled it well. The suspect got rid of the evidence, that's all.''

"And we don't have a case on him."

"Nothing from the vacuum bag?"

"Clean."

Wager shook his head. "He's dealing and we know it. We'll get him next time."

The sergeant poked out his half-smoked cigarette in Wager's unused ashtray. "Robbins claims he was beat up. He's got bruises in the groin area."

"He climbed out a window. Maybe he got his balls hung up on the sash."

"Come on, Gabe!"

"Ed, it was dark, the suspect was trying to escape, and there was a little scuffle."

"The unit can't afford any sadists, Gabe."

"Will you take my word?"

"Sure. And so will Sonnenberg."

"All right. Denby had nothing to do with it. Robbins was a bad break but it's not that big an issue. If it had been me that blew it, nobody would say anything. And I could have blown it as easy as Denby. Hell, Charlie Masters was there—he didn't get anything either, did he?"

"No."

"All right, then. Give Denby a fair chance; we'll learn soon enough if he fouls things up."

"You sound sold on him."

"All I'm saying is give him time; last night wasn't a fair test. And Jesus knows we're short-handed right now."

"Right. I'll pass the word to the Inspector. Anything on that Seattle tip?"

"I'm going out there today."

"Keep me posted."

Two minutes after the sergeant left, Denby poked his head around the doorframe. He looked worried. "I saw you and the sergeant talking. I thought I'd wait outside."

"It was about you and Robbins. I told him it was the same bad luck that could happen to me or to him or to anybody else."

"You really think so?"

Wager looked at him sharply; he had no patience with

28

grown men who whined. "I do."

"Well." Denby cleared his throat. "Well, we'll get him next time. You want some coffee, Gabe?"

It was after lunch before he could get clear of the office to go out to the Rare Things Import Shop. At the West Thirty-eighth Street ramp, he swung his dark green Dodge 650 off the freeway and onto one of those streets widened years ago from a neighborhood road to a through avenue. Now it was crammed with cars and traffic lights, and though many of the homes and tenements lining the curbs still had old-fashioned curtains at their windows, most were becoming shops and stores. Wager drove slowly down the shimmering street and felt the relaxation that comes with the sense of fitting in completely. It wasn't his old neighborhood—that had been scraped away by the bulldozer blade—but it was close enough to it so that when he parked and stood a few moments in the white heat of the sun, he had the sensation of going back in time: of seeing himself as a bony-kneed kid sprinting down these same sidewalks, of knowing already what kind of people would be in the stores, how they would greet each other, how these streets would fill in the cool of evening, and how the invisible back yards of the sagging houses were patched with cool, worn clay in the shade of cottonwood trees.

He sighed and walked the half-block to the Rare Things. It was on the north side of the street in one of the newer buildings, a low rectangle whose front showed three or four doors flanked by plate-glass windows. One window was soaped with a "FOR RENT" sign, and someone had sprayed "The Chicano Army is on the move" in paint across the concrete block. Next came an auto-parts store, then the import shop, and beyond that the last store, which bore a sign for unpainted and refinished furniture. Cheap. On the corner, a stark house, whose yard was now treeless and filled with white gravel for a parking lot, was the Cantina Bar. That brought a faint memory, and Wager dredged it up: a shooting incident in late summer, 1971, three kids—two brothers against a third Chicano—one dead, one still in Canyon City. A question of manly honor. Or sister's honor. Or just plain showing off.

He paused in front of the import shop's window and studied the empty doorway with its Chamber of Commerce sticker and the red "OPEN" sign, then the display of tumbled bolts of East Indian cloth, a big brass tray, heavy Spanish candlesticks, paintings of bright colors and heavy outline: *"Ojas Altas en Mazatlán,"* a burro and cactus, a big-chested señorita with a water jug on her head. The shop seemed empty of customers and help; no faces peered back through the reflections gathered on the glass, no shapes moved in the dark of the store. He pushed into the air-conditioned coolness, heralded by a bell whose tinkle sounded unused, and stood waiting.

From somewhere in back, a low murmur of voices suddenly stopped and a clerk came through the beaded curtain: five feet ten, around twenty-five years old, black hair, brown eyes, Chicano, no distinguishing marks or scars. "Can I help you?"

"I'm looking for some Spanish chairs. The wooden kind."

"We don't carry much in the furniture line. Mostly decorations and souvenirs. You might try next door."

"Do you sell enough of that for a good business?"

A deprecating shrug. "We do all right. Maybe we'll go into furniture soon."

"Are you Mr. Montoya?"

The smile went away and the boy's brown eyes flattened into suspicion. "Mr. Montoya, he ain't here."

Wager could feel someone listening intently from beyond the bead curtain over the back doorway. Moving casually along the front of a dusty glass case filled with ceramic pots marked *"hecho en México,"* he peered over the boy's shoulder. The shadow of a man waited just beyond the door. "I thought I heard you talking with somebody when I came in."

A pause. "That was my uncle. Mr. Montoya owns the place but my uncle and me manage it."

"I see. I wanted to talk with Mr. Montoya. You know where I can reach him?"

"Maybe you better talk to my uncle."

He disappeared, and after a short whisper the waiting figure pushed through the curtain and around the glass case, brown eyes laughing at Wager's attempt to hide his surprise. "Gabe! After all this time! It's good to see you."

30

There it was: the silent electric quiver, the click of two scattered things snapping together.

"Rafael!" Wager let his hand be taken in both of the other's, and wondered as he smiled if he had changed as much as Alvarez. Where, as a teen-ager, Rafael had been as slender and smooth-faced as his nephew, he was now growing heavy along the jaw, and the lines at the corners of his mouth and eyes had the carved look of permanency. Three years in jail would give him the lines; too comfortable living would flesh out his chin.

Alvarez leaned back to look up and down. "No uniform? You still with the plainclothes detail? Hey, Anthony, this guy's from the old neighborhood—now he's big time in the police. Come on in the back, Gabe. Have a cup of coffee . . . maybe a drink?"

The walk was like the old Rafael's, one shoulder hitching slightly higher than the other as if ready to throw up a defense; and once again Wager had the feeling of having been moved back in time. "How long have you been here?"

"Over a year now. Almost two. Hey, this is a real surprise!"

Wager looked around the small office and took the padded seat Alvarez pointed to. It had the feel of a home rather than a place of business: the worn cloth on the overstuffed chairs, the scattered and filled ashtrays, the magazines, and even a small color television in the corner panning across an emerald infield spotted with tiny white figures. "So you're in the import business now," Wager said.

"It's a good living, Gabe, and an honest one. Like I tell Anthony here—he's my sister's boy—honesty's the best policy. *Hombre*, I sure have learned that!"

Anthony smiled and looked embarrassed. "The Cubs are leading six to two," he said, and turned the sound off so the two men could speak. "It ain't much of a game." Wager liked the boy's manners.

Rafael tipped a shot into a small glass and pushed across a covered dish of lemon slices and a salt shaker. "Here, a little José Cuervo."

"*Salud y pesos.*" Wager lifted the glass and touched his tongue to the salt.

"*Amor y besos,*" said Alvarez, laughing.

31

They swallowed and bit into the lemons in silence. Alvarez waited.

"Business seems slow," Wager said.

Alvarez's eyes narrowed in another laugh, and he nodded at the younger man. "Anthony's always saying that, too. He wants to get rich quick. But business is really pretty good," waving a laborer's broad hand over the desk crowded with envelopes and catalogues. "We do a good mail-order business. To gift shops and things." He offered Wager a cigarette and apologized, "I forgot you don't smoke," when Wager shook his head.

There was another silence, and finally Wager said, "I'm not with the burglary and stickup division any more."

"Oh?" Alvarez's hand slowly balanced his cigarette over the ashtray.

"No. I'm with the Organized Crime Division now. The narcotics unit."

"That so? That's a promotion, I guess. Gabe's a smart man, Anthony. From patrolman to detective in—what is it now—six years?"

"Seven."

"Que tiempo ha pasado! It seems like yesterday you were on the burglary detail. You remember when Gabe busted my house, Anthony?"

The young man's eyes glided without blinking from his uncle to Wager with some of the puzzlement replaced by a harder interest. "This was when you worked construction?"

"Right on—Gabe's the man. There I was, sweating my *talangos* off for two dollars an hour and when I come home, what do I find! My whole house a mess—drawers emptied, beds upside down, some dude crawling through my attic with a screwdriver, wife and kids crying, supper not cooked, and there's good old Gabe, cool as a cucumber in the middle of it all!" He laughed again, the gold fillings of his teeth catching light from the low ceiling. "Gabe had this big idea that I was handling stolen goods or pot or something. Maybe you even thought my kids were fencing, eh, Gabe? But good old Gabe didn't find a thing, because there wasn't anything to find. But Holy Mother what a mess! It took my old lady a week to clean it up. Another drink?" He pushed at the bottle with his polished fingernails.

"No, thanks."

"I ask you, Anthony—you're a smart boy—would I be doing peon work for two lousy bucks an hour if I could get rich without working?"

"He's the one you took the picture of?"

"Hey, yeah—I forgot about that. Remember, Gabe? I even took a picture of you standing with the wife and kids." He winked at Anthony. "It ain't every day you get visited by a bunch of real live detectives."

"I think I'd of been pissed off." Anthony stared at Gabe.

"What for? There was a search warrant—everything was legal. Gabe had a job to do and he did it. It's in his blood, like. He was just wrong is all. Mistakes happen."

"What happened at the border a few years ago?" Wager said.

A shadow crossed Alvarez's face before he shrugged and smiled again. "Another mistake—mine this time. I shouldn't have done it; it was dumb. But no more, brother, no more. I learned: you play with fire, you're gonna get burned. Now I'm straight."

Wager looked around the office, at its plastic imitation wood paneling and standing lamps. A serape with banderillas hung on one wall, and the shelves of a small bookcase were filled with straw vaqueros and wood carvings of a skinny Don Quixote. "This is a real nice place. It must cost a lot to get set up like this."

"Honest work, Gabe—and lots of borrowing. It's sort of a family thing. You know, the uncles and cousins—they invested."

"Is Montoya a relative?"

"A distant cousin—by marriage."

"You think it's any of his business?" Tense anger had replaced the young man's politeness. Wager wasn't just a cop, but worse: a Chicano turned cop.

"Anthony! What do we have to hide? Honesty is the best policy, and if you got nothing to hide you got nothing to fear." He smiled apologetically at Wager. "He's young . . . believes in that machismo stuff. It's in the blood, you know."

Wager nodded and stood up. Anthony, an inch or so taller, looked down at him with masked eyes. Rafael stood, too. "You leaving already?"

33

"I have to get back to work."

"I thought you wanted to see Montoya?" The eyes laughed again. "Or buy some furniture."

"Not any more."

"Oh. OK—well, *hombre*, it's good seeing you. And any time you're in the neighborhood . . . you don't need a search warrant here, OK?"

Wager sat a few moments in the car to let the impressions settle. Something was going on; he felt it in Alvarez's words, his smile, the feeling that Alvarez had been waiting for some kind of investigating officer, had rehearsed what was to be said, and then found himself relieved and even amused that the officer turned out to be good old Gabe Wager. And—despite the caution—Alvarez had been unable to keep the slight note of challenge out of his voice, as unable as Wager to forget the childhood competitions, the taunts that signaled victory or jealousy, the constant efforts to outdo each other. But this wasn't childhood, and these games, if no more serious, could be far more deadly. Anthony. He seemed like a good boy. But there was something about him, too: not just defensive, but aggressive and personal. In his eyes, Wager wasn't just Cop; he was also Enemy. And yet still basically a good boy, new to his uncle's game, giving some fancy political or psychological name to what he was doing so it wouldn't sound like what it really was. Maybe even some college education, so he wouldn't have to think but could just pin labels. *Cachaza, amigo, cachaza! If* he was dealing, suspicion wouldn't convict—it took evidence.

Wager jotted the information on a contact card and then let his pencil follow his thoughts. Little or no business and a perfect front for shipping stuff across the border: notify postal authorities and customs for routine surveillance of mail with the Rare Things address. Probably nothing hidden on the premises; Alvarez would move the stuff out fast when it came in. If it came in. Storage. That much grass would have to be stored and then packaged: a warehouse somewhere else. And a family business. That would be tough: a tight organization would make it impossible for an outside informant to work his way in. Yet if it was that big, that well-organized, they should have heard of it; a lot of cannabis was on the street, but Alvarez's name wasn't linked to any of it. Something was

34

wrong there. But something was going on; Wager felt it. And whatever it was, Rafael felt safe enough to offer him a drink and to show that he was laughing at him.

Cruising slowly past the shop once more, he turned right at the corner and right again, through the narrow tar-paved alley that ran behind the building. The rear doors were unmarked and had once been painted pink. A sign bolted to the bare concrete block said "CUSTOMER PARKING ONLY—RARE THINGS IMPORT SHOP—VIOLATORS WILL BE PROSECUTED BY THE LAW." A nice touch, that, pure Rafael; Wager smiled to himself and pulled into the square of crushed gravel dusted with bottle chips and tufts of wiry grass. A car sat scalding in the sun: red-over-black '73 Firebird, Colorado number AS 3101. On the front seat rested a Panama hat; the back seat had the clean emptiness of a new car. Something was going on. No windows at the rear of the store, though the pink door had the tiny bead of a peephole, and Rafael was probably staring out at him and splitting a gut right now. Across the alley was someone's back yard guarded by a slat fence, with the redwood boards broken and sagging here and there. Anyone sitting on the other side of the fence could be easily seen. The west end of the alley behind the Cantina Bar would be the best place for surveillance.

On the way back to the office, Wager radioed for the owner of the license number; it was registered to Alvarez, address 655 West Eighth, Denver. Another tiny click. He called Suzy's number, and in a couple of seconds her thin voice radioed back, "This is two-one-six."

"What was the address of the owner of the Rare Things Import Shop?"

"Wait one." He could picture her flipping through the yellow folders until she came to it. "Six-five-five West Eighth."

"Thanks. Ten-twenty that address."

"Ten-four."

He remembered the house when he saw it: brown brick, squarely built, with the front porch a deep shadow across the first floor, the second floor rising in a peak. White wooden pillars, needing paint, lifted from stubby brick bases on the porch. The last time he'd stood here, Alvarez's wife, pale with shock and anger, had stared numbly at the warrant he'd held. But now the house was empty of kid noises, almost empty of life. The screen door, thick with old patches, rattled as he knocked. Finally, an old man's face peered out between the tassled curtains masking the small pane in the door; then a lock grated open to show a thin figure shorter than Wager's.

"Yes?"

"Mr. Montoya?"

"Yes?"

"Are you the owner of the Rare Things Import Shop?"

The rheumy black eyes widened a little, and Wager felt the old man's sudden worry. "I own it. But I don't work there none. I'm too old now."

"Does Rafael Alvarez live here?"

The worry deepened. "Who are you?"

He showed him his badge. "Detective Wager. Does Rafael Alvarez live here?"

"No, sir. He moved out south. On Monaco." Under the sagging chin of his scraped neck, a thin Adam's apple bobbed once or twice. "Is there some kind of trouble?"

"His car is registered to this address."

"I don't know nothing about that. He moved maybe six months ago."

"Did you run the shop before Alvarez took over?"

"Yes, sir. Eighteen years. We moved to that new store in 1965." His dark eyes slid past Wager and stared at some vision against the thick shade of the elm trees. "That was before my wife, Sadie, died. Business was better at the old place. That new store"—he shrugged and shook his head—"it's too far out of the way."

"Don't you have a good mail-order business?"

"Mail order? I never mail-ordered nothing. It ain't that big of a store. For mail order, you got to have lots of stock and storage space. And clerks, if it's big enough. And capital to get started —that kind of business takes a lot of mail advertising."

"You don't have a warehouse?"

"Warehouse? Ain't no warehouse. Just the store."

"How long has Alvarez had the business?"

"He came about a year and a half ago, and then took over when I retired. He's a smart young man. He'll do good in the store."

36

"You retired six months ago?"

"Yes, sir. Just after my wife, Sadie, died."

"At the same time Alvarez moved from this residence?"

The Adam's apple bobbed again.

Wager let the silence work for him.

The old man's hand, knuckles bony under the wrinkled skin, tugged at the curling tip of his white collar. "Yes, sir. We made a kind of . . . agreement."

"Like what?"

"He lets me live here and I let him run the store for the profits."

"You don't pay him a salary for managing the store?"

The collar was tugged again and the worried eyes shifted to defensive embarrassment. "I couldn't pay him nothing. I was going to close the store, and he said he'd manage it for the profits and let me live here rent free in trade. I . . . I needed a smaller place after my wife, Sadie, died."

"Did you sign any papers?"

"No. Did I have to?"

"I guess that's up to you."

"I mean, was it against the law not to?"

"Not that I know of—it's your property. Is Alvarez making a profit now?"

"I don't know. I don't go by the store no more, but it never did too good since we moved there. Maybe it is now, though. Rafael was willing to gamble on it, he said, and he's been able to take care of the overhead and taxes, anyway."

"That was a pretty good deal: a free manager and a rent-free house."

"It wasn't my idea! Rafael said he'd do it; he said he needed to learn how to run a store and he was willing to gamble on the profits. The store's still in my name. We never signed no contract to trade anything anyway, and if he wants out he can leave tomorrow. We never signed no papers and there ain't nothing in the law against it. You said so yourself!" The thin folds of flesh quivered under his jaw as he stopped for breath. "Business is business!"

"Do you know Alvarez's new address?"

"I got it wrote down." He disappeared into the dark living room, and Wager heard a drawer slide open. Then the short

37

figure returned reading from the back of a business card, "1123 Monaco Parkway Circle."

"Thank you, Mr. Montoya."

"Say, is there something wrong at the store? Something I should know about?"

"Not that I know of."

"Why all these questions, then?"

"Just checking out the car registration." Alvarez would get a call from the old man five minutes after Wager left, but it wouldn't hurt for him to worry some. Worry was good for the soul. If you had one.

In the car, Wager noted his talk with Montoya and called Suzy to let her know he would be in the office by four-thirty.

"Detective Denby says Willy has some more action."

"Pat and Mike?"

"Yes."

"Ten-four." Fat Willy was using up his free dope fast. He was probably cutting it again, for a little profit off the high-schoolers, and maybe Wager should care a little more about that. But he didn't, not really down deep. If the little bastards wanted to shoot up, nobody could stop them, and their lunch money might as well go to the good cause of nailing pushers. At this rate, they'd be able to set up Pat and Mike by next week; another week and then Willy'd be hungry again and cruising the streets to sniff out another pusher.

The Monaco Circle address was in one of the many new residential suburbs where streets curved around each other, and only signs such as "Prairie Wood" or "The Downs" or "Partridge Hills" separated one sprawl of homes from the next. Alvarez's was a split-level: entry, living room, and dining room on the ground floor; bedrooms and baths up half a flight over the garage; basement—probably finished—down half a flight beneath the living room. Lot, location, and building about, Wager guessed, thirty-eight thousand. Plus a hot new car. Not bad for a laborer two years out of prison and running a store that had no customers. But the fact that a man had money didn't mean the money came illegally. Or so the courts would say. Click-click-click, pieces of the puzzle were coming together here and there. But one big fact still didn't fit: it would take a lot of marijuana to provide that

38

much money; and nowhere had Wager heard Alvarez's name linked to marijuana. Or to anything else.

From his desk at the office, he called the DEA and asked for any information they had uncovered from the Seattle tip.

"Not much, Detective Wager. With the case load we have, we're sticking to the hard stuff. Are you on to something?"

"Only a little." He gave the deskman his information.

"Right, I remember Alvarez. It sure sounds like he's dealing, doesn't it? But we don't have a thing on him, and right now we're too jammed up to free anyone for a new investigation. Maybe by the end of the month . . ."

"I understand."

"If you want, I'll alert customs and they can check any shipments coming from across the border."

"I've already done that." He hung up as Denby came in.

"Did Suzy tell you we've set another buy from Pat and Mike?"

"I heard," said Wager.

"You think we should set up surveillance?"

"No, it makes Willy nervous and there's no reason to take a chance on being seen."

"OK." Denby blew his nose and muttered something against ragweed. "What did you get on the Import Shop?"

Wager went through it one more time, talking as much to himself as to Denby, lining up the information and weighing it once again.

"Don't you think there's enough for a search warrant now?"

"It's still so-so; it'll depend on the judge. But it wouldn't do any good. He doesn't keep the stuff on the premises. I've been through that with him before." It had not been a pleasure, that time five years ago, when, hot with the chase and blindly certain of his information, he had broken into Alvarez's house, sending his wife on a crying jag and seeing the wet-eyed hatred of the children as they watched the raiding team tear through every drawer, strip the beds, probe cushions and mattresses, scattering worn underwear and frayed toys, dislodging and clumsily chipping the plastic Madonna. And stupidly finding nothing. Not one damn

39

thing. Wager had been very lucky on that, he knew; Alvarez could have raised holy hell, but he didn't. Probably because he really did have a stash somewhere. But it had not been a pleasure, either, standing before the district chief to be chewed out for finding nothing—being shown graphically how much more difficult it would be for him to get subsequent warrants when a search was unproductive. Counterproductive. That was the word the chief had used: when a search was counterproductive.

"Well, you're the one who knows. I got a lot to learn. I guess I showed that last night."

It was a conscious effort at humility, and it rubbed Wager wrong—as if Denby were wagging his tail, hoping to have a pat on the head. And Wager couldn't bring himself to feed Denby's self-pity. "You do," he said.

Denby hung around a few more minutes, said good night to Suzy, whose heels clattered through the rapidly emptying offices. Finally: "It's after five. Going down to your car?"

"In a little while. I want to think about this Alvarez thing."

"Any action tonight? Other than the Pat and Mike buy?"

"Not a thing."

"Well, Helen'll be glad to see me on time for supper."

"Take it easy."

"See you Monday."

The outside door closed behind Denby, cutting off the buzzer's rattle. Wager stared through the window at the hot afternoon sunshine that blotted out the details and colors of the mountains. Beyond west Denver's stubby skyline, almost out of sight in the hazy distance and the green foam of scattered trees, lay what was left of District 3, with its tired brick tenements and sagging frame houses. Rafael Alvarez. It brought back the district's smell and sound and the powdery touch of crumbling brick that reddened your clothes when, as a kid, you rubbed against the walls to chase a ball or another kid. Rafael Alvarez had been one of the chasers and the chased. So had Gabriel Villanueva Wager. At that time as children, and later as cops and robbers, and now once again. It was enough to make a fatalist of you.

He unlocked the small door leading upstairs to the attic and
40

the cardboard boxes that held inactive files. There it was, dusty now, and smelling of old copy paper: "Alvarez, Rafael (none) DPD#75862, b 15 Sep 1943; 15 Jun 65 arr possession marijuana, probation 1 yr; 30 Oct 66 arr suspic burglary, no convic; 4 Apr 69 arr Nogales, Ariz, smuggling marijuana; 16 Jul 69 sent 2 yrs El Reno Fed Pen; serv 14 mos incl time await trial; 15 Sep 70 parole; no other convic. Residence: 655 W. 8th, Denver."

He crossed out the old address and put in the new Monaco Circle one. Then he pulled a manila folder from the storage cabinet, carefully inked Alvarez's name and DPD number on the lip, and placed the file in the active drawer.

4

Three weeks passed before Wager found a few minutes to pull the Alvarez folder again. This work was, he thought, like a virus: when action started in one location, it spread for some reason across the cases until every time he was on his way to one corner of the city, two or three informants were trying to call him from other areas. And then came periodic calms, like now, when it seemed that every pusher in town slowed for breath, when it seemed that the virus had used its strength and was waiting to gather more energy before starting another run. Maybe it had to do with moon phases, or biocycles, or—if anything—periodic shipments coming in to major suppliers. Whatever the reason, there had come a pause and Wager finally had time to answer the itch of the Alvarez file.

"Suzy, did Detective Denby say when he'd be out of court?"

"No, he just said he'd check in."

Because Denby's face was still new in the area, he had seen a lot of recent use as the arresting officer for local and federal agents; now the busts were starting to appear in court, and Denby spent more time as a witness than as an officer on the street.

"What about Ashcroft?"

"He's on loan to the Pitkin County sheriff's office."

"On loan again? How long's that supposed to last?" It was a dumb question. It would last as long as it had to.

"I certainly don't know!" She still resented his tone when he was irritated, even though she knew he wasn't angry with her. And that fed his anger more.

"Is Sergeant Johnston in?"

"He just came out of the Inspector's office."

Wager knocked on Johnston's doorframe and waited until

43

the balding man looked up. "Come in, Gabe." Johnston said. "You've been pretty busy lately."

Nodding, Wager sat and did not hide his disgust. "All little stuff—street buys, that kind of thing."

"Not much to brag about, but it's got to be done."

"It takes up time, Ed. And people. Ashcroft's up in Aspen, Denby's in court every goddamned day, and we still don't have a replacement for Simpson. I have cases that I haven't been able to look at for three weeks, and when I get to them, all the people are loaned out. When do we get enough people to do our job?"

The sergeant leaned back and looked at him narrowly. "When's the last time you had a vacation?"

"You've been watching the goddamned *Late Late Show* too much—don't go psyching me out, Ed. I've got a case I want to get some consistency on, and it's going to take a team. Now we don't even have our own people to work with."

"Which case?"

"Alvarez—the Seattle tip about that import shop."

"Do you have anything new on it?"

"How can I get anything? That's what I want the team for!"

"What does DEA have?"

"Nothing. They're tied up, too. I asked customs to watch for any shipments coming through from Mexico, but there hasn't been a damn thing."

"Tips?"

"Nothing."

Johnston stared down at the forms on his blotter and then up again. "You don't have any hard evidence?"

"Something's going on, Ed. The guy's got a record for dealing, he's living high with no visible income. And he's not working the street. He's on to something, and it's got to be behind the street."

"Gabe, if we get some slack I can maybe help you out; but until that happens or until there's some real evidence, I can't justify the expense. This new line-item accountability system those half-wits saddled us with doesn't give me any flexibility. You get me some solid corroborating evidence, and I'll do what I can to get the money. But in the meantime, I've got

44

to prioritize the operations, and the priority standard is the probability of conviction.''

''What the hell does all that garbage mean?''

Johnston reddened and Wager knew he'd struck a nerve; the sergeant liked to use administrative language. ''It means, goddam it, that we spend our time on sure things!''

''Well, our TO calls for a replacement for Simpson. The money's budgeted—do we have a man coming or not?''

''The money *was* budgeted. There's a freeze on positions and we *don't* have a man coming.''

''Jesus Christ! Whose side's the legislature on?''

The anger was gone from the sergeant's voice, and it was steadily patient again. ''The Inspector says he's asking for a supplemental appropriation to get the money back. We should know in a few weeks. In the meantime, I've got to keep assigning cases on the maximum probability of conviction.''

''OK, OK, I understand.'' Wager sighed and stood. ''What's coming up?''

''For you? Not a thing right now. If you want some time off, take it now. God knows you got it coming.''

Wager shrugged. ''Maybe I can find some of that corroborating evidence.''

The sergeant laughed. ''It won't do us much good right now, so don't look too hard.''

''I can't hear you.''

''How's Denby working out?''

''Fine, I guess. From what little I see of him.''

Wager went back to his quiet desk and sat a few moments, gazing but not really seeing the walls crowded with framed certificates and posters. The Law Enforcement Code of Ethics was tacked to the wall over Simpson's empty desk; it said a policeman should be a good guy. Around it were smaller frames that said being a good guy wasn't good enough: Colorado Law Enforcement Training Academy; U.S. Department of Justice—Bureau of Narcotics and Dangerous Drugs National Training Institute; International Narcotics Enforcement Officers Association; Law Enforcement Award; Letter of Appreciation from . . . . He pulled out his notebook with its cryptic symbols of informants' names and jabbed one of the unlighted buttons on his phone. Dial-

45

ing, he waited and counted the rattles of the bell at the other end of the line. Finally, a sleepy voice mumbled hello.

"This is Wager. I want to see you."

Squawk.

"I want to see you tonight at the Frontier. Six o'clock. Be there." He hung up and dialed another number from the little book.

"Ray? This is Gabe. I need some help."

"How much help?"

Some you threatened, some you bribed—with money, with self-importance. "It could build up into something hot—it could be real important. Have you heard of Rafael Alvarez?"

A silence, and Wager could picture the gray face dusted with white bristles as it twisted in thought. "Alvarez? I don't know . . . there's a lot of spicks around." He added quickly, "No offense intended, Gabe."

"None taken." To the spicks he was a honky, to the honkies he was a spick. It used to make a difference; now, screw all of them.

"Alvarez? No. What's he into?"

"Marijuana."

"Funny I ain't tumbled on him."

"He's supposed to be big. As high as a thousand pounds a week."

Ray's low whistle sounded choked with an old man's phlegm. "That's some brick pile. I should of heard of anybody that big. Unless he's got a special market. Maybe he just transfers?"

"The word is he wholesales."

"I should of heard of him if he's that big. Funny."

A lot of people should have heard of him if he's that big. "Let me know if you find out anything. If I'm not around, leave a message with Suzy."

"Who?"

"The secretary. She'll take messages for me."

A long silence as the face probably worked again. "I don't know. I don't like too many in on this."

"Do you trust me or not, Ray?"

"Yeah! You're all right . . . but . . ."

"She's all right, too. You're part of a big operation, and Suzy's part of the team, too."

46

"Oh. Well, I guess it's all right." The sound of a cigarette shoved between his lips followed by the faint crackle of a match near the receiver. "Alvarez? Supposed to be big in pot?"

"It might mean some real bread for a change."

"I could use it for a change."

He tried one more number, but there was no answer; perhaps it was just as well— it was dangerous for an informant to ask instead of just listen. Old Ray would know that, and Leonard—the CI he would meet at six—wouldn't stick his neck out for his own mother unless he was kicked. Wager wouldn't have to sweat either of those two.

Denby burst in, a glow of pleasure in his blue eyes. "Gabe, we got the bastards! I bet they're hit with five years! The bench even congratulated the prosecution on its case."

' "What was the defense?"

"Mistaken identity—they thought it was the defendants' word against mine for identification. Shit! They should have pleaded guilty—what they didn't know was that Billy and another DEA man were watching the whole thing with glasses. Positive identification from three sources. Shit, man, you should have seen their faces!"

"That's fine. It's nice to see the good guys win one."

"Yeah. It feels good. And we're going to nail some more, too. Billy has another case starting tomorrow on that bust up in Louisville. You know, the one where I chased the bastards down when they saw it coming."

"That's going to be tougher."

"The dope was in their car."

"I heard it was a question of proper search."

"Aw, crap, no. They showed it to me before they started to run. Billy says we got them nailed."

"Sure you have. When the hell are you going to be through in court?"

"Gee, I don't know, Gabe. I'm the main witness, you know. Billy says he'll need me for all the hearings as well as the trials. You got something lined up?"

"I'd like to get on with the Alvarez thing."

"Oh, that. Well, as soon as I'm through, let's get to him. It may be a week or two, unless you want to do some night work. You want to bust him tonight?"

47

"On what? I need a case before I can bust him. I need some goddamned surveillance!"

"Oh. Well, I don't know. It may be a week or two."

"I guess I can handle the preliminary stuff myself."

"I'll be real glad to help you out at night when court's not in session. Just let me know so I can tell Helen."

"I'll do what I can myself."

"Right on. Man, you should have seen that defense lawyer's face!" Denby's excited voice filled the office so that Wager barely realized Suzy had answered the phone until she called his name.

"It's for you, Gabe."

"Detective Wager speaking."

"I got a meet tonight with Pat and Mike. I'll need some bread for it." The voice wheezed with the effort of heavy flesh.

"This is number four, Willy."

"Sure, man, I hear you. Is your man ready? What's his name?"

"Denby. He's right here."

"He ain't used up, is he?"

"He's been working out of town."

"I don't want no fuck-ups. I don't want no snitch jacket on me."

"There isn't one big enough, Willy."

"Aw, yeah. Here's the deal, man. Have this Denby dude meet me at Fifteenth and Champa, at the Woolworth's. Eleven-thirty tonight. We go down the block for the meet. I told them he just wanted a little bit."

"That's good for a start. We'll be there."

"*He'll* be there. I don't like crowds."

"You sound strung out, Willy. What's the matter?"

"Just you do it my way or it's no way."

"Woolworth's, eleven-thirty. You're on."

Denby leaned over the desk as Wager hung up. "Pat and Mike?"

"Right. Fat Willy told them he's bringing a friend."

"It's about time. Say, it'll be good to be number-two man, for a change. We'll have those two broads in a week."

"In three or four weeks. We want a solid felony charge."

"Right. You gonna back me up?"

48

"I'll be around, but not too close. Willy's really up tight about something."

"Think he'll stay legitimate?"

"I think so, but it's always a question."

The younger detective was quiet a few moments. "That puts some pressure on the number-two man, doesn't it?"

So far, Denby had been the number-three man, the arresting officer supported by backup people; now he would have to cover Willy and meet with the suspects all alone. The job was just becoming clear to him.

Wager stretched and folded his hands behind his head. "You'll have to string Pat and Mike along by yourself for a while."

"How up tight did Willy sound?"

"He's real nervous. But it could be about anything. Maybe he needed a fix."

"Yeah, maybe. Could he get nervous enough to tip them off about me?"

Wager shrugged; it could happen. It could always happen. And Denby had a right to know what he was getting into. "He knows where his bread comes from, and he's never finked before."

"Yeah. But there's always a first time."

"That's so."

"Well, what the hell; that's what I'm getting paid for, ain't it?"

"That's so, too. But I'll be around for each of the meets."

"Good. But I can't help thinking of that broad covering the action with a pistol."

"If Willy tips them, they just won't show up. They're not looking for a fight."

"You never had a phony tip from somebody out to waste you?"

"I have." More than once, if you're lucky.

Denby nodded and sighed. "Eleven-thirty tonight?" He blew his nose. "I better tell Helen. She had a movie in mind."

"I'll see you about eleven."

"Right." His voice sounded a bit forced.

It was dinnertime at the Frontier and Rosy's face shone

with sweat as she hustled among the tables, her arms loaded with hot dishes from the kitchen. In the afternoon, she had a relaxed freshness and there was time to swap a few words, but by now there was only energy enough for grim efficiency. Like her life. Three kids and a skipped-out husband whose only good deed, she said, was leaving. Wager went down the row of crowded tables that dully reflected the chandelier made from an old wagon wheel. No Leonard. He sat at the end of the bar and waited.

"Hello, Gabe, how's by you?" Red, the bartender, still had an Eastern note in his voice.

Wager nodded and ordered a draw. "Business all right?"

"Too good," Red said, slapping an icy mug on the bar and meticulously wiping up a circle of old beer. "Hot-weather drinkers—can't keep up with them." He bustled away to the other end of the bar to answer the flapping hand of a customer coming in the door. The bartender knew he was a cop, had smelled it on him, but he never poked into Wager's work. Which was why Wager kept coming back.

Halfway through the second beer, he saw Leonard come in: shorter than Wager, Chicano all over him, with straight black hair, and shoulders bent to keep the rest of the world away. His face was thin despite the full cheeks and the drooping mustache. He answered Wager's nod with a glance and sat at one of the back booths.

Wager carried his beer over. "Hello, Leonardo."

"What the hell do you want, Wager?"

"Rafael Alvarez. What do you hear of him?"

Leonard tapped a cigarette on the plank table. "I'm goddam tired of you leaning all over me whenever you feel like it."

"My friend," said Wager with his gentlest accent, "I own you."

"Hi, there." Rosy materialized from the dark and Wager ordered two more Coors. They sat silent until she brought the frosty steins. Leonard lit a new cigarette from the stub of the first and jabbed the old one out in the cluttered ashtray. "You fuckers," he said bitterly. "Fuckers like you always own people like me. Someday you'll get yours."

Wager sucked at the cold beer and waited. Finally, Leonard ground out his cigarette and reached for his beer.

Wager said, "Alvarez. You remember Rafael. He's supposed to be a big supplier of marijuana. Uses an import shop for a front."

"More power to him."

"I want you to find out how straight that word is."

"Bullshit—I'm not sticking my neck out!"

"You either stick your neck out with him or you stick it out with me."

"You don't have anything on me."

"I'll get something on you."

"Goddam you, I been clean!"

"You won't look clean when I get through."

"You son of a bitch." He buried his mustache in the beer foam and glared at Wager.

"If you want to make a buy, I've got money."

"I don't want nothing from you."

Wager shrugged. "It's cover."

Leonard was silent and Wager saw him weighing it; they both knew how it was going to end, but there were certain steps to go through first. Leonard was still struggling to keep a little bit of something like pride wrapped around his useless life, and for a moment Wager almost liked the dumpy figure pinching himself together in stubbornness over the beer mug. But only for a moment.

"How much?"

"We'll start with a brick," Wager said.

Another silence. "I don't like it. I've heard some things. . . ."

"Like what?" Wager moved too quickly.

Leonard's dark eyes mocked him. "You're really hungry, ain't you? Yeah." He lit another cigarette and leaned back against the tall wooden seat back. "I'll buy you a little grass."

"I want it from Alvarez."

"What difference does it make who it's from?"

"It makes a difference."

"He might not be handling it, Wager."

"What have you heard?"

"Nothing. Not one fucking thing."

"This might be big, my friend. I want some information."

Leonard shrugged. "I'll buy you some grass."

"What have you heard?"

51

"What do you want Alvarez so much for?"

"What have you heard?"

"Nothing!"

Wager counted out four tens and let Leonard see him mark it down in his small notebook. "If it doesn't come from Alvarez, don't buy."

"I'll see what I can do," Leonard said sullenly.

"Call me tomorrow night. Nine o'clock."

"I can't get anything that soon!"

Wager smiled. "OK, I'll be generous. Make it eleven."

"Goddam you, Wager, I can't even make a contact that soon!"

"You hustle a little, my friend. Or you'll have a vacation in colorful Cañon City."

Even in the dimness, he saw Leonard's face pale so that the drooping mustache looked black against his lips. "They'd kill me."

"I know. Eleven. Tomorrow night."

"I can't do it, goddam you!" The bravado was gone and the dark eyes were stretched with terror. There was something; Leonard knew something he was still holding back.

Wager drained his mug and pressed the moisture from his mouth with a paper napkin. "I don't see why not. If Rafael's got it, he'll want to sell."

"I haven't heard of him dealing in marijuana."

"What have you heard of him doing?"

"Nothing. His name just comes up every now and then, but nobody really knows what's going on."

"What have you heard, Leonard?"

"Just that he's in fat city somehow. That's all the word that's on the street: Rafael's got it made. New car, new house—that shit. But nobody knows what he's doing—it could be marijuana or it couldn't be."

Wager shook his head when Rosy paused to ask if they'd like another round. "See what you can buy, anyway."

"I'll listen around."

The summer sun had finally dropped below the mountains, throwing their shadow across the shallow bowl of the sprawling city. Above the glass towers of Fourteenth Street, a jet blasted across the sky, its wing lights beginning to glow in the dusk; then it was gone, a rush of engines fading through the tall buildings. Wager shoved further into the small box around the pay phone and tried to blot out the noise as he dialed. It rattled five times before Ray's wet voice answered.

"This is Gabe. You find out anything?"

"If this guy's dealing in grass, I'd know. And he ain't."

"Nothing at all on him?"

"He's known, but I couldn't get no leads."

"Who knows him?"

"Well, it's kind of funny—a lot of people. But nobody knows what he's doing. Or they won't say nothing. And a couple of the spicks was real nervous about saying anything about it."

"How?"

"You know—like I shouldn't of been asking. And maybe I shouldn't."

"Any problems?"

"Naw, they was just surprised-like that somebody was asking."

"Well, keep your eyes open and play it cool."

"Hell, yes! I don't want to collect no shivs. With niggers it's razors, with spicks it's shivs."

"So I've heard."

"Yeah. Anyway, something's maybe going on, but nobody's saying much."

As Wager paid his car out of the parking lot, he checked his watch and turned north on I-25 to cruise past the Rare Things. The windows were dim, but a glow inside meant someone was still in the back room. Wager turned past the tavern and up the alley. Alvarez's Firebird was behind the store; beside it was a white-over-dark—maybe dark blue—Caprice '71, Texas plates CVM 389. He thought, but wasn't sure, that the county code meant El Paso. Down the alley and left through a residential block, a U-turn without lights, and back to the alley to park in the narrow band of darkness against the building wall. He reached under the seat to where his transmitter rested in the mobile pack, took it out, and called the Texas number into DPD for a check. In a few minutes, the reply came back: "No warrants issued." He sat for half an

53

hour or so watching the back door, finally giving in to his stomach and driving until he saw the glaring yellow arcs of a hamburger stand; back again, this time parking across Thirty-eighth and adjusting the rear-view mirror to frame the Rare Things' front door. He settled down, bit into a tasteless hamburger, and, eating slowly, sipped now and then at the coffee whose heat had gone to leave the faint flavor of paper cup. Eating was something to do when you sat and watched; eating made time pass. At 9:38, a dark Mach-1 Mustang, Colorado plates BC 3226, parked in front of the store and Alvarez's nephew Anthony strolled in. On the contact card Wager listed the Mustang and plates under the previous Texas entry. At 10:15, the inside lights went dark and a couple of minutes later Anthony came out and drove west on Thirty-eighth; Wager swung left at the corner and parked at the entrance of the alley in time to see the Firebird and the Caprice back away from the building and also go west. Wager marked the time and event on the contact card and completed the routine by calling for a check on Anthony's license number.

"Registered to Rafael Alvarez, 1123 Monaco Parkway Circle, Denver. No warrants."

"Thanks."

A new car for nephew Anthony—gift of Rafael, whose store did little business. After finishing the entry on the card, Wager scraped together the crumbs and wads of paper from his lap and the car seat and crushed them into the paper bag; then he went past the dark store once more and headed downtown to meet Denby.

Denby had changed from light sport jacket and tie to Levis and a denim shirt. "How's it look? It's what I been wearing as number-three man. Is it all right?"

"Legitimate. All you need's the patchouli oil."

"Ha-ha." He looked puzzled. "What's that?"

"A perfume some of the hips wear."

"Oh. You think this'll be good enough without it?"

"All they have to do is see you. They don't have to smell you."

"Oh. Ha-ha."

"Don't let Willy know that I'm in the area."

"Right. What about my hair, think it needs to come down this way more?"

"It looks fine."

They went to the graveled parking area beside the OCD offices. Denby slid into his own car, rolled down the window, and called to Wager, "You have any ideas where you'll be?"

"Probably around the corner on Fifteenth. I'll follow you."

"Roger."

Downtown traffic away from Capitol Hill was a brief pulse of surging cars filled with young faces still excited by the movies that had just let out. Wager circled the block on the one-way streets and pulled into a no-parking area in front of a skin-flick marquee. The young, clean-cut kid behind the tiny window peered at him nervously over the paperback book he pretended to read. Wager saw Denby's car pass the red Woolworth's sign once, turn left and then right down the block; a moment or two later, Denby's voice came over the radio: "He's on the corner, I'm picking him up now." Wager clicked his transmit button twice to acknowledge and slumped down into the shadow of the seat. The blue Fury III went past the intersection slowly, with a large white-coated figure in the rider's seat. Wager let a few cars get behind Denby's, then pulled into traffic. Ahead, the Fury turned right out of the mainstream of traffic, and Wager turned behind it; seeing it cruise slowly north, he turned right and sprinted through a red light to parallel the blue car, turning back toward them on the next one-way street. When he glimpsed the Fury turning in to an alley just this side of Larimer, Wager eased his car, lightless, to the curb beside the dark heave of a demolition project. A minute—at the most two—later, the Fury backed into the empty street from the alley and headed west; Wager followed in silence until he saw Denby pause at the curb to let Willy lift himself out. Then he keyed the mike: "Did it go all right?"

Denby's voice, mixing excitement and relief, came back: "Right! Real fast—she almost didn't stop to count the money."

"OK. I got an evidence bag; I'll see you at the DPD lot."

"Right."

Denby was there ahead of him, angling through the enclosure crowded with police vehicles and civilian cars. Wager pulled in at the curb and walked to Denby, who dangled the balloon at him. "Here we are!"

"Fine. Let's get it in the locker." He had Denby fill out and sign the first entry, then walked with him to the locker where a baggy-eyed policewoman initialed the time and her receipt of the evidence and placed it in the safe. In the morning, a lab tech would initial the evidence out, check its substance, record it, and initial the evidence back in, where it would wait until the prosecutor needed it—the chain of possession carefully recorded on the cover of the brown bag.

5

Another week passed before Ray called in, a week when the action picked up with the same viral effect Wager had noted earlier. The word came in that Spider Robbins was in action again; and Fat Willy had dropped out of sight, which meant he had some deal going. The surveillance of Alvarez had become a routing of stops at the Rare Things and the Monaco Parkway address, but there were no new facts, no hard evidence. Simpson's old position was still unfilled, but Ashcroft was finally back and following up the calls left by his stable of CIs; Denby had bought another balloon from Pat and Mike, this one alone, and his early excited worry was replaced by faintly swaggering self-confidence: "Those broads"—he shrugged—"no problem." Wager wondered briefly if there was something wrong with himself; Denby offered a choice of personalities and Wager couldn't seem to like any of them.

"What do you have, Ray?"

"Can you meet me at the Gaucho's?"

"When?"

An old man's wet cough into the mouthpiece: "Half-hour."

"I'll be there."

It was a Larimer Street bar where water stains blossomed through the low ceiling of fiber panels; the bartender called them "gaucho marks," but Wager couldn't see anything funny in it. They just matched the rest of the beat-up décor: peeling asphalt tiles and tables that tilted wearily this way and that. Wager ordered a small draw and waited at the bar until Ray came in, his chalky face touched bright pink on the cheeks, limp white hair across the dome of his bony skull.

"Let's sit back here."

Wager ordered two more beers and followed the thin figure to the darkest of the many booths.

"You don't smoke yet, hey?" The old man pushed a

57

quivering filter tip between his narrow lips as Wager shook his head. He dropped his voice to a mumble and leaned across the table. A faintly bitter smell rose from its sticky surface. ''You was right about this Alvarez—something's going on. But it ain't grass. It's bigger.''

''Coke? Smack?''

''Smack.'' He rumbled a cough and spit a wad of something on the wrinkled floor. ''He's pretty big in it, but I ain't sure how big.''

''Where'd you get your information?''

''Well, I got to thinking, you know, about all the grass the guy was supposed to be handling. Anybody that big in grass I should of heard of. So I think maybe it's something else, you know. And I put out the word I'm looking for some hard stuff, that my customers is shifting off grass.'' He smiled at Wager apologetically and shrugged. ''A little grass never hurt nobody, and I got to have cover.''

''It's legal if you don't get caught.''

''Yeah—that's what I think, too. Anyway, I ask around for some stuff''—he paused to cough again and rinse his mouth with beer—''and this black dude says he can put me on to it so long as I give him a broker's fee and stay out of his territory. Which ain't no problem; I wouldn't last a minute in Five-Points.''

''Who was it?''

''A guy named Spider Robbins—you know him?''

''Roland Robbins? About six two, skinny and mean?''

''You know him. Anyway, he says, 'I can put you on to some fifty-percent stuff.' ''

''You want to do it?''

The thin shoulders rose and fell. ''I ain't never been in on anything this big before.''

''I'll get the money for you. Where'd you say the stuff was coming from?''

''That's what I'm getting to—I asked him was it good stuff and all that, and he says it comes in from Mexico and they cut it here. It's a local product, he says, satisfaction guaranteed. I says real fast, 'Yeah, I heard that before—give me a local name,' and he says, 'Ever heard of Alvarez?' 'He's in grass,' I says; and he nods like this, real slow, and I says, 'Put me on it, I'll see you in a couple days with the money.' ''

"That's all?"

"I wasn't going to push him any more, Wager."

"OK. When'd you talk to Robbins?"

"Just before I called you."

Wager let the information settle and felt more pieces of the puzzle shift and click into place. There were a lot of gaps and as yet no solid evidence, but the shape was beginning to rise out of the growing collection of facts. "How much do you want to buy?"

"I don't know—a couple ounces, maybe. I don't want to come on too strong at first."

"Right. Check with me tomorrow and I'll have the money." He pulled three twenty-dollar bills from his wallet. "Here's a down payment on the tip. I think you've got something this time. If it goes all the way, you could clean up."

"Hey, that's real good!"

Wager drove to a pay phone and dialed Leonard's number, telling the surly voice to meet him at the Frontier in twenty minutes. As usual, the soft-faced kid was as late as he thought safe.

"I've been waiting to hear from you. You were supposed to call last week."

"For Christ's sake, let me get a drink first."

Wager ordered a bourbon and water for him. "What'd you buy?"

"Jesus Christ, you pigs are all alike!" The drink came and he shoved his mouth at the glass. "I didn't make a buy. I just ran across the name."

From the small kitchen window a voice called "Number three," and Rosy trotted up to carry away the plate of burritos and refried beans. "Who'd you hear it from?"

Leonard didn't bother to answer. "He used to handle grass, but he don't no more."

"Since when?"

"Since he quit! Jesus, you want me to fix up a calendar now?"

"I don't want you pulling me through the grease, friend. I want facts I can check out. Since when!"

59

"Since I don't know when. Maybe a year, maybe more. The street says he used to deal a little and a year or so ago he stopped delivering. That's all."

That would explain the confusion from the Seattle tip; it could be that this Eddie Hart, whoever he was, had spilled his guts about everything he ever heard—every whisper, every rumor—in an effort to lighten the sentence or to help him score as an informer. Rumors, facts, lies, inventions, all mixed up in a scared mind trying frantically to wheedle the best deal—a thousand miles away from the facts. "How little's a little?"

"A little!"

"Twenty pounds a week? Fifty?"

"I don't know—I swear to God I don't know how little's a little! It wasn't a lot, that's all." He thumped the heavy-bottomed glass on the bar and beckoned to Rosy for another. "Jesus, my stomach! You're killing me, Wager, and I hope to fuck you get yours someday."

Wager smiled. *"A cada capillita se le llega su fiestacita."*

"What the fuck's that mean?"

"You wouldn't understand it in English, either. Who'd he sell to?"

"The street—anybody who wanted it. Baggies, lids; I guess he wasn't in it long enough to get a route. He could of built up if he stayed, maybe—it was good stuff: Mazatlán gold, Acapulco red. But he quit."

A Mexican connection; relatives, maybe, or contacts among the braceros he worked with. The marijuana flown in or driven over the border five or six hundred pounds at a time and spread out to half a dozen middlemen, who in turn supplied their street men. Wager could trace the network in red, green, and yellow lines with key airfields and ports of entry underlined on the customs map framed on the wall of his office. "Who supplied him?"

"Come on, Wager, you know better than that."

"Names, Leonard, did you hear any names? Who'd he run with?"

"Nobody said and I wasn't about to ask. It was a long time ago."

"Why'd he quit?"

"How the hell do I know? Maybe there was too much

60

competition—it's a pretty crowded business, you know. You guys just can't keep up with it, can you?'' Leonard smiled, an ugly sight Wager hadn't seen in the three years since he first busted the pusher. ''What are you looking at?''

''Leonardo, sometimes I almost like you. Almost.''

''What's that mean?''

''Never mind. Here.'' He slipped a five-dollar bill on the bar and stood up. ''Pay for the drinks out of that.''

''Five? What the shit, Wager, you said this was worth something!''

''What have you given me, my friend?''

''Well, you said it was worth something!''

''It's worth something if you give me something. I handed you forty bucks last time for nothing. All you tell me is that he's not dealing in grass any more; I can't get any convictions on that.''

''Goddam you, Wager. I stuck my neck out asking questions—I mean some people really wanted to know why I was asking questions!''

''Like who?''

''Never mind.'' Leonard turned back to the drink.

''If Alvarez isn't dealing, then you didn't stick your neck out. If you find something, you get paid; no information, no money.''

Silence.

''You get me some information about Alvarez. He's up to something and I want you to find out what it is.''

''Goddam you, Wager, I told you all I could find out.'' He rubbed at his stomach and spit part of the drink back in the glass. ''Goddam!''

''I'm betting you can find out something more, Leonard.''

''Get somebody else; leave me out of it.''

''You want bread, you give information.''

''There ain't no information!''

Wager leaned down and murmured toward the ear nestled in bushing sideburns, ''I hear he's heavy in heroin.''

Leonard's soft face jerked back, dark eyes wide. ''You didn't hear that from me!''

''I should have, *amigocito*.''

The eyes blinked twice, three times. ''You son of a bitch.''

''Think about it—you say people knew you were asking

questions. I can put out the word I heard it from you."

"You son of a bitch."

"Or I can give you some cover."

"You set me up!"

"You're goddam right I did. And if you don't produce, you are dead. Cold dead. You check in with me in three days with some solid information or the word goes out about our meet tonight." He left Leonard staring at the cloudy ice cubes in his drink, a sour expression on his face, from his stomach or from Wager or from both.

Wager had over two hours before meeting Denby for the bust on Pat and Mike; he drove down Thirty-seventh Street and into the alley behind the Rare Things. Alvarez's car sat by itself in the dim twilight, and he turned right and right again to slip into a parking place down the street from the store. Scattered neon signs glowed here and there: small, functional, probably turned off as soon as the shop closed. Only the bar at the other end of the block would glow all night. Wager couldn't see the bar itself, because it was set back from the sidewalk, but glaring light from its sign and porch fell across the pavement in a patch of cold yellow. Slumping down in his seat, he turned the volume of the radiopack down to a murmur and watched. Nothing: no one going in, no one coming out; no Anthony in his hot Mach-1; no Texas plates that might be a link to the Mexican connection. If there was a Mexican connection. Heroin came in from a lot of different directions: California, New York, Canada, the Gulf Coast. And Mexico. He flipped through the notebook and keyed his microphone for DPD: "Can you check customs and immigration for this license number: Texas, CVM 389."

"Roger. Wait out."

The dusk slowly changed to a night that was slightly chill with the first hints of coming autumn, but still warm enough to bring out strolling couples and clumps of hooting, laughing kids, full of supper, excited by the lateness of the daylight, moving, always going someplace where the action was supposed to be—somebody's big brother buying a six-pack, and then around a corner to get higher on excitement than the beer could ever lift you. And then moving again to wherever the action was by now. Because it was always just ahead of you.

62

He, Rafael, and so many others like the kids who now walked, laughing and loud, past the car. What had happened? Where did they go? Except for Rafael, the others were ghosts; and Wager, too, often felt like a ghost. How did young Rafael end up a dealer? How did Wager end up a cop? And why in the quiet moments did the past seem more real than the present?

"Two-one-two."

"Go ahead."

"They both said to call back in the morning."

"Ten-four." He should have known: regular hours for nonessential personnel. He gave the store a few more minutes but it was quiet; then once more through the alley and a quick meal before locating Denby at the office.

"Where's the meet?"

Denby was in his Levis and denim shirt and smelled of patchouli oil. He looked up from the report he was drafting. "Over on the east side. You know that parking lot in front of the zoo?"

"That's wide open; it's going to be hard to bottle them up."

"I've got some help."

"Billington and Masters?"

"Masters and somebody else. Billy's on loan out of the county."

"Just those two?"

"That's all I could get."

Wager shook his head, "It's a lousy place. Well, let's get set up early."

"Masters and his partner are on their way. We'll meet them there."

Denby and Wager cruised across the deserted black asphalt of the zoo parking lot, under the scattered arc lights. Concrete planters filled with low shrubs divided the area into long empty rows and separated the lot from the boulevard running between the black of the golf course and the bulging shadows of the zoo grounds. From the darkness of the zoo came the grunting cough of some large cat and an occasional wailing squawk.

"Jesus, what's that?"

"I think it's a peacock."

"It sounds like Helen yelling at the kids." Denby keyed the radio. "Two-one-nine, you set?"

"Yeah."

"Two-one-ten?"

"All set."

Denby sighed with nervousness and blew his nose. "Now we wait awhile. Jesus, that golf course must be full of ragweed."

"You have the money?"

"Oh, yeah. Here." He handed Wager an envelope thick with soiled, marked bills.

"How much is it for?"

"Four ounces. I said you were in from the Western Slope."

Wager counted the bills—$1,000—and initialed the transfer form. Then, for the next half-hour, they sat wordless but alert, studying the occasional car that sped down the boulevard, listening for footsteps, waiting for the radio to click its warning. Finally, Denby looked at his watch again. "It's about that time. I wish we knew where Annie was sitting."

"We'll probably find out soon enough."

"No shit—that's what worries me!" Denby drove once through the parking lot, then turned around in the boulevard and came back to the entrance. They stopped near the glare of one of the tall lights and waited; Denby turned down the radio volume. "She said eleven. It's quarter after now."

"They're probably checking us out."

"I better let her see me." He strolled in front of the car, pausing at the thick shadow of low shrubs in one of the dividers.

Wager heard a crunch in the gravel; a slender figure came toward them from the boulevard. They must have come across the golf course. Annie would be covering them with the pistol or Labelle wouldn't be coming in. He clicked the transmitter three times, then turned it off. Denby went toward the figure, paused, beckoned to Wager.

"This dude says you want to buy." Labelle's eyes were narrow with suspicion.

"I'm ready to deal."

"How's things in Pueblo?"

"I'm in from Steamboat." 64

"I thought Fred here said you's from Pueblo."

"Steamboat. You want to deal or not?" He looked around at a passing car whose headlights flashed across them. His nervousness was real: Annie was probably in the shadow of that spruce tree by the entrance, and in the light Labelle just might remember his face from six years ago.

"How much you want?"

"Four."

"I got more if you want it." She patted the woven purse at her hip.

Wager said, "I got money for four. Maybe more next time."

"I thought you said he was a heavy."

Denby shrugged. "That's what he told me."

"You don't want all that I got in here?"

"I only got money for four this time."

Labelle's teeth flashed white. "Good thing you answered right. I be back in a minute." She disappeared behind a screen of shrubbery. Denby and Wager stood in silence until she came back, a small white paper sack in one hand.

"Let's see the merchandise."

"It's good."

"So's my money." He opened the bag and unfolded a paper to check the color and taste. "You're right—it's good. Here's the bread." He waited until she began counting it. "All right, sweetheart, it's a bust. We're on to Annie, too, so don't make things worse."

The woman's eyes whitened and she leaned back holding the half-counted wad of money away from her. "You fuck-ing pig!"

"Don't do it, Labelle—we're on to you!" He flashed his chrome-plated .45 and held the evidence out of her reach.

"You pig! You ofay pig!"

Wager yanked the handcuffs from his belt and twisted the squirming arm up behind her back. "Pick up the money, Fred. Get over here, you bitch!"

"You motherfuck, you finked on me—you set me up! I'm gonna kill you, motherfuck!"

Wager spun her toward the car and pushed her across the hood, rapidly slapping at her body for weapons while the skin on his back puckered and he hunched against the expected shot. "Come on, come on!" He hustled the woman into the

65

safety of the car and sighed involuntarily.

"Don't blame Freddy, Labelle. It was him or you." He called into the transmitter, "Two-one-two—suspect in custody."

"We got Halsam."

"Glad to hear it. See you downtown." He sighed again and locked the car doors. "Come on, Freddy, I'll give you a ride downtown."

The car was silent until they neared Capitol Hill. When Wager pulled over to let Denby out on a corner near unit headquarters, Labelle leaned forward, shoulders pinched by her handcuffed arms. "Freddy, I'm gonna remember you. I'm gonna remember you good, baby."

Denby said nothing.

"You son of a bitch!" she screamed. "I'm gonna see you again, Freddy, you son of a bitch!"

The younger detective shut the door. "Have a good evening, mama."

At DPD, Wager saw Charlie Masters completing his file on Halsam. "Any trouble with Annie?"

The black detective's hard eyes studied Labelle's face and body. "Naw, we got her before she could scratch her ass." He pointed to a tagged .38 Smith & Wesson. "She had it but she didn't want to use it."

"Where'd you put her?"

"Room three—see you in a while."

Wager tagged Labelle's pistol for evidence and set it beside Annie's. "His and hers! Hey, Labelle, honey, which one's his?"

"Fuck you, pig."

Wager had the grinning property man count and sign for the thousand dollars. "OK, let's go talk."

"Fuck you, pig."

"Don't take it so hard, honey; we'll put you in a woman's prison—all the pussy you want." Wager set her on one of the hard, upright chairs in room 2 and flipped on the lamp. "You want the cuffs off?"

Silent; eyes full of hatred shadowed by wiry hair.

Wager adjusted the lamp so it was in her face and unlocked the handcuffs. "Here's your rights, Labelle." He spoke the familiar litany from memory and then sat across the empty

66

table from her. "It's a felony charge—three to five, maybe five to ten." He smiled. "In a different prison from Annie." He let it sink in. "But you do me a favor and I'll do you one."

"Like what?"

"Like telling me who your supplier is."

"What supplier?"

"You haven't left town in weeks, Labelle. Somebody's bringing it to you. Who is it?"

"Ain't nobody brought me nothing."

"If I don't get a break, you don't get a break."

"Yeah! Fuck off."

"You don't owe nobody. Why cover for anybody?"

"I don't owe you."

"You owe yourself, baby. You'll be in a long time, and little Annie will be outside all by her lonesome."

Silence.

"Annie's not going to wait around for five years. Nobody would."

"You motherfucking pig!"

"It's up to you. We'll find out sooner or later. You want to get something out of it while you got the chance."

"I don't want shit from you."

He felt someone come in behind him and stand in the shadows: one of the uniformed officers bored with night watch and dropping by to see what was going on in interrogation. "We've got all night."

No answer. Her sullenness grew in the glare of the desk light, and Wager studied the deep lines of her face—lines not from laughter but from weariness, worry, and age. Not so long ago, she, too, had been young, a little girl with bony knees and pigtails and big dreams, and what had happened to her? And why? He stretched and stood; there wasn't time for answers to such questions—not even time to ask them. She wasn't a little girl any more; she was a criminal and a tough one.

Behind him, the officer scratched a light for a cigarette and watched with bored curiosity.

"I need some coffee—keep an eye on her for a minute, will you?"

"Sure."

In the hall, Gargan, the police reporter, stopped him.

"What'd you pick up, Gabe?"

"Just a routine buy and bust. Nothing big."

"Like what?"

"Four ounces of cut stuff. Nothing big."

Gargan scratched somewhere beneath the collar of the turtleneck shirt he always wore. "Anything lined up?"

"Nope. We're always trying, but we don't have anything big yet."

"Let me know if something breaks?"

"Will do."

He filled a porcelain mug at the coffee urn and stopped by room 3, where Annie sat framed in light, her back to the door, a small ring of officers standing or sitting in the shadows around her. "Anything?"

Masters shook his head. "She claims Labelle handled everything. Says she never even saw the stuff."

"Crap."

"Sure it's crap. But we do not wish to violate her Constitutional rights as a pusher. Besides, she didn't have a thing on her except the weapon. How about you?"

"Not a thing. Labelle's tough."

"I bet she is!" The big man stepped into the hall and yawned and rubbed his bloodshot eyes. "I think Annie's a possible if they're kept apart."

"The matron can handle that."

"We can turn her around in a while."

"I hope so." Wager waited a moment, then: "Do the Bureau files have anything on a dude named Alvarez?"

"Man, you got as many Alvarezes as we got Willy Joneses."

"Rafael. About thirty-two, busted once for transporting marijuana. Now works at an import shop on the north side."

"Can't place him. What do you have on him?"

"Nothing yet. I'm trying to get enough for a team surveillance."

"I'll let you know if we turn anything up."

"Thanks."

A corporal called down the hall, "Wager? We got a Detective Wager here?"

"Here."

"Phone."

"Coming." He stuck his head into room 2. "I'll be right back—I have a phone call."

"Yeah? Well, this is supposed to be my coffee break," the officer said.

"I'll do you a favor sometime." The dumb bastard should have taken his break like everybody else: in front of the television watching the New York police catch all the criminals. Or was it Thursday? If it was Thursday, it was the Los Angeles police's turn. He picked up the receiver resting on the night desk. "Detective Wager."

"Hi, Gabe. Denby. How's it going?"

"She's full of kind thoughts for you, but that's about all."

"She thinks I'm the snitch?"

"Right—our man's covered."

"How about Annie?"

"Masters thinks he can work her around. She was clean, but we can get an accomplice charge. And a concealed-weapons charge."

"Think I can get any part of her?"

"Better stay clear. We want to keep our man covered while he's still useful."

"Yeah. Damn. No good at all with Labelle?"

"Nothing. She's been this route before."

"Damn. I sure need to build a string of snitches."

"We'll get some for you."

"Yeah. Well, Helen's calling me. I'll see you in the morning."

He went back to room 2 and waved the uniformed officer out of the interrogation room. "I got her now."

"Some coffee break!"

"Thanks for the help." And next time keep your goddamned nose out of other people's business.

The woman sat motionless in the hard light.

"You're not hurting anybody but yourself, Labelle."

"That's the story of my life, pig."

Wager yawned a bit wider than he had to. "It's your fanny, honey. I'll see you in court." He called the matron.

"Hey, piggy, one thing—you tell that Freddy somebody gonna be looking him up."

"But, baby, it won't be you. Not for a real long time."

The yawn had been half true; he was tired. Behind the sting

69

of his burning eyes he felt weariness spread in his mind, and one by one his senses lost their edge until, as he closed the car door, he had the familiar woolly numbness of exhaustion. He started home, his body already hungry for sleep; then, with a curse, he turned north instead of south when he came to the Valley Highway. If he didn't do it, nobody would: one quick swing past the Rare Things before bed.

The alley was almost black—few of the store owners replaced the lights constantly being broken by stray rocks—but the parking area was crowded with four cars nosed against the import-shop wall. He recognized three: Anthony's, Rafael's, the Texas plate. The fourth—a tan Pontiac Le Mans '72, Colorado AF 1306—he called in. It was registered to Henry O. Alvarez of 3422 Kalamath, Denver; DPD checked the name for him and came up with file number 159319 and a middle name, Obregon. No warrants. Rafael's older brother. The weariness faded with the interest of finally seeing something happen, and Wager parked across the street from the store and watched the front. At 12:53 A.M., a dark-colored 1971 Buick Skylark, BC 7130, parked in front of the building and two males—Chicano, medium build, one dressed in a suit, the other in the Levi trousers and jacket of a bracero—knocked on the glass door. Anthony let them in and locked the door behind them. Wager noted the information and called for a make on the license: Francisco Xavier Martinez, Apartment 6, 800 Thirtieth Street, Denver; Dalewood Apartments. Denver Police Department had no file number for that Martinez. He tried to dredge the name up in some connection with the papers and references in the Alvarez folder. Nothing. At 2:03 A.M., the two men came out, one carrying a grocery bag, got into the Buick, and swung around east on Thirty-eighth. A few moments later, Wager saw the cars from behind the store turn on to Thirty-eighth at the end of the block. The deal was over. He let Rafael's Firebird go two or three blocks down the empty tunnel of streetlights, then followed. He knew where Rafael was going; he could see it on the city map he carried in his head, and he even drew a mental circle around Rafael's home. He knew exactly where the suspect was going, but he was cop enough to have to be certain. Rafael turned south on Valley Highway at a moderate rate of speed, and finally took the Evans Avenue turnoff

70

east to Monaco and home. Wager wrote the time in his notebook and, fighting the weariness that was coming back much stronger now, like a heavy tide, he drove north to the Martinez address to tie in that one loose thread. It was an aging brick apartment set just off a thoroughfare and tucked under heavy trees that lined the slabs of red stone walk. The white columns on the porch and the bay windows reminded him of a poverty-stricken old lady trying to keep up appearances—and succeeding if you didn't look too close. He debated searching the mailboxes for the name but decided against it; he was too tired. Francisco X. would have to wait until morning.

6

Wager arrived at work late, but there had been little sleep for him. Despite his weariness, he had spent a night rolling and twisting hot in the sheets, trying to stop his mind from bringing up ideas about the Alvarez case. Ideas about old evidence, possibilities of new facts, areas for more investigation. And the old memories that sprang from his contact with Alvarez: faces, places, the undefinable sharpness of something one still remembers and for no reason at all—the fuzzy skin and the new shoes smell of the chapped baseball they used for one long summer series of sandlot games. It was one of those nights that seemed to come more and more often the older he got, and they always left him more exhausted than if he had given up trying to sleep and just read all night. And, worse, sleeplessness for no real reason; he and Rafael hadn't even been friends. By accident they ran in the same bunch, but there was never any *compadre* feeling. And it was a long time ago. Business was business, he told himself; he shouldn't lose sleep over a criminal who was old enough to know the risks. If one runs with wolves, one starts to howl, he told himself in his grandmother's voice. But it had been a lousy night despite what he told himself.

"Gabe, Inspector Sonnenberg wants to see you."

"What about?" Even to him, his voice sounded harsh.

"Well, I don't know!"

"I guess I'll find out if I go see him, won't I?"

Suzy did not answer, and he patted her shoulder in awkward apology as he went to the Inspector's office.

"Shut the door, Gabe."

He took a captain's chair and waited. Sonnenberg lit a maduro with one of the long fireplace matches he kept in a glass on his desk. "I hear Denby's doing pretty well lately."

"Yes, sir, he's been in on several busts, and last night

73

played the snitch on Pat and Mike. He did a good job."

"Everything went OK?"

"Yes, sir."

The Inspector studied the slowly growing ash of the cigar. "I had some doubts about the man, and I'm still not a hundred percent on him. There's something"—he wagged his hand, palm down—"I don't know. For all his time in uniform, he still doesn't *smell* like a cop."

Sonnenberg was talking more to himself than to Wager, and though he knew exactly what the Inspector meant, Wager kept his lips shut. A man doesn't bad-mouth his fellow officers. To a superior, anyway.

And Sonnenberg knew that, too. "Well, I'm pleased he's turning out well. I want you to make sure he's in on as much as possible; we want him thoroughly trained as soon as it can be done. Our unit's getting some flak from a few of the uniformed divisions who think they're losing income to us, and by God I want to be able to tell the Joint Budget Committee that we're not wasting the taxpayers' money."

"Yes, sir."

The cigar tipped up. "This Pat and Mike thing, how big is it?"

"They're third-rate heroin pushers. We only went after them because they were set up."

Sonnenberg's pencil drummed against the metal lid of his round address file. "Anything else?"

"The Seattle tip looks like it may be worth something." He brought the Inspector up to date.

"Your informant's certain Alvarez is dealing in heroin?"

"He hasn't bought any himself yet."

"Then it's just in the rumor stage so far."

"Yes, sir. But that's where they all start."

He nodded and gently scraped the ash from the cigar into a ragged gray curl. "What kind of support do you need?"

"Twenty-four-hour surveillance on Alvarez; systematic surveillance on the Rare Things. If it looks hot, I'd like to go to a full team plus a wiretap."

The Inspector slowly flipped through the pages of a green logbook and shook his head. "I can't spare anybody right now, Gabe. The entire OCD is up to its ears with this Texas

74

Mafia crap, and we're supposed to provide investigators for three grand juries—two here and one down in Pueblo."

"How about outside support? There's people who owe us favors."

"That's the Lord's truth. But we don't have enough evidence yet to justify a request of this size." The pencil tapped again. "I'll tell Sergeant Johnston to hold you off new assignments so you can dig into this."

"Yes, sir."

When he got back to his desk, Suzy had a message from the laboratory. "They said Browne's heroin was thirty percent."

"Is that all? It was supposed to be fifty!"

"They said thirty."

That was a second cut. Labelle was either ripping off an extra profit or she had bought when she should have boogied. "Has Denby called in yet?"

"No."

"When he comes in, tell him I'm down talking to Labelle. And ask him to phone customs and immigration for anything they might have on this license." He gave her the Texas number and then dialed Ray, telling the old man to meet him in the Civic Center park. "Oh, and Suzy, get a copy of DPD file 159319, Alvarez, Henry Obregon."

Sergeant Johnston issued the cash for Ray's buy. "The Inspector says you might have something from the Seattle tip."

"I hope so, Ed. It feels pretty solid so far."

"He wants Denby on it with you when he's free."

"I know." He signed the form without looking up to see the grin he knew Johnston would have.

"Good luck."

He didn't want anybody's sympathy, with or without a laugh. "I can always use that."

The gray concrete benches in the park matched the sky, and a dry autumn wind sent scraps of cellophane, leaves, and dust scratching along the broad walk between the formal plots of yellowing grass. More than the cold, it was the grayness and the scraping sound that made Wager shrug deeper into his topcoat with an odd feeling—half pleasure at the emptiness of the park, half discomfort at its bleak sameness. Near the semi-circle of concrete pillars, he found the old man bundled against the wind and pinching his cigarette stub for warmth.

"Hello, Ray."

"Jesus, it's colder'n a well-digger's ass."

"We're the weather capital of the world."

"Yeah—we get enough of it."

"Here's the money; you'll find a little extra in there."

"Hey, swell!" He slipped the envelope unopened into his frayed coat and stood up. "You mind waiting awhile before you leave?"

"You worried about something?"

"Yeah, well, I ain't never been in on nothing this big before, and I guess it makes me nervous. It don't hurt to be careful, anyway."

"I'll give you five."

"Yeah. I'll call you when I get something."

He watched the short figure, with its collar turned up to the windblown white hair, walk stiffly past the columns of the monument. Ray was right, it didn't hurt to be careful; but there wasn't really that much for him to worry about, either—it was a straight buy. He'd been around enough to handle something like that.

In the cold, the five minutes went slowly, but a promise was a promise; Wager watched the clusters of assistant DAs bustle up the Civic Center steps, the distant Grey Line buses unload tourists to stand in shivering lines at the gates of the Denver Mint, the strings of yelping schoolchildren guided by harried teachers toward the rippling walls of the new art museum, whose scalloped architecture still made him feel a little uneasy. A museum should look like the box it was, holding the things people want to go stare at; but this false-front thing just didn't look like a museum. It looked like a make-believe castle where the builder wanted everybody to know it was make-believe, so he stretched it some here and there. Wager liked things to look like what they were supposed to be, like the capitol over there with its big gold dome and the long lines of columns that said government.

Slowly the cold of the concrete bench worked through his trousers, but he gave it another couple of minutes. Then he walked the two blocks to the office parking lot. Denby was just getting out of his car as Wager arrived.

"Hi, Gabe—holy shit, was I tired! I must have been more wound up than I thought last night." He pinched his nose in the handkerchief and blew. "Man, is it dusty!"

"The Inspector wants us to spend some time on Alvarez. I'm on my way to see Labelle now. How about checking this license out with immigration and customs?" He wrote the Texas number on a leaf of his notebook.

"Sonnenberg thinks there's something in it?"

"He's interested but that's all."

"What's with Labelle?"

"She sold us a quarter cut."

"No shit! Man, if you can't trust your pusher, who can you trust!"

"Maybe we can get her for false advertising. See you in an hour."

The woman waited at the small table, face drawn and sagging with fatigue; the scrubbed gray prison smock hung baggy from her shoulders. Wager nodded good morning to the matron, a thick-bodied black woman with flat, expressionless eyes, then sat across from the prisoner. "Hello, baby."

"Well, well, the spicky piggy. You come offering another deal?"

"I thought a good night's sleep might brighten your outlook."

"Good night's sleep—shit!"

"Don't hurt the taxpayers' feelings, baby; this is a style to which you will get accustomed."

"Yeah."

"I want you to look at something. It's a lab report on the smack you sold me."

She stared suspiciously at the cryptic form, her lower lip moving as she read. "So what's all this shit?"

"It says you sold me a quarter cut."

Her bloodshot eyes widened slightly before she could guard against surprise; then she laughed a harsh bark. "You gonna arrest me for cheating?"

"If you paid full price, you got ripped off."

She stared again at the lab report. "A quarter cut, you say? Ain't that just like a fucking greaser!"

"Who's that?"

77

"The dude who sold me. I'll tell you this much—what's your name, Wager? What kind of name's that for a greaser?—the dude that ripped me was a Chicano kid. I wouldn't be surprised if that motherfucker Freddy wasn't Chicano, too."

"Why cover for this kid? Why not get even?"

Labelle's humorless laugh came again. "Go out and work for your money, piggy! Even a rip-off artist is better than you!"

On the way back to the office, he mulled over the obvious connection: it could be the same pipeline for Labelle's supplier as for Alvarez. Or it might not be. Best to hold the pieces close but still separate until something else turned up to link them together. Better to wait and be sure than to go running headlong down the wrong trail. Slowly, slowly, one step at a time.

And that was how he went up the office stairs; Mrs. Gutierrez waved good morning from behind her plexiglass window and pressed the buzzer to open the door to the inner offices. Denby was waiting.

"Immigration had nothing for that license, but customs did. It belongs to a Richard Valdez, aka Ricardo, Dick, Fuzzy; 13228 Houston Avenue, El Paso, Texas."

Wager copied the address into his notebook. "Do they have a jacket on him?"

"They got one, but it's going to shake you." Denby smiled and waited until Wager said "What?" "It turns out this Valdez is one of customs' top snitches for the Juárez zone. They don't want us going near him."

"Barbas tienes! Did you tell them he might be transporting heroin into Denver?"

"No. I didn't know if you wanted that out yet."

"You're right, good thinking." He picked up the telephone and dialed, "This is Detective Wager. Is Agent Hartnoll in, please?"

"Hi, Gabe, what can I do for you?"

"Howie, we're working on something that might touch one of your Concerned Individuals: Valdez, Richard—from El Paso."

"Fuzzy Valdez? Yeah, I know him; I've used him a couple of times. He's really reliable."

"Have you ever heard of him dealing?"

"Nothing big. He may bring a baggie or two across, but you know how that goes."

"I know. Listen, I've got something confidential here. We think he's tied in with a heroin ring in this area. His car was seen last night at a meet. Is there any way the El Paso people can get some information on him? Where he's been, who he runs with—that kind of stuff?"

"Fuzzy? Heroin? You sure?"

"The car belongs to him."

"He's one of our best informants. He only touches pot."

"The car checked out, Howie."

The line was silent a few moments. "Man, he's reliable. I'd hate like hell to lose him. Let me make a couple of calls and I'll get back to you. You at your office?"

"Thanks, Howie. And don't let this information get too far."

Denby's eyebrows bobbed query and Wager shook his head. "He'll call back in a little while."

"Gabe?" Suzy came in, her cheeks still red from the cold wind. "Here's the other Alvarez file you wanted."

"Thanks, Suzy. Let's take a look at this; it's Rafael's older brother Henry." He and Denby sat and studied the Xeroxed pages, Wager adding occasional lines to the small notebook he was beginning to think of as the Alvarez journal.

"He spent some time in El Reno, too. Just after Rafael. It must run in the family."

Wager grunted and took a careful look at the small list of known associates. No Francisco X. Martinez, no Fuzzy Valdez. Two convictions: one for burglary—suspended, first offense—and a two-year rap for transporting marijuana. It was the usual slim jacket on a small-time crook.

"Think you can find out from the El Reno authorities who the Alvarez brothers ran around with?"

"Sure—if anybody remembers."

"Give it a try."

Denby dialed long-distance information while Wager started through the papers once more, filling in Henry's life from his own memories. The addresses, the names, even the dates created echoes: popular songs, sport names, the really important news of the district—Father Heinmann being replaced by the first Hispano priest, Father Lopez; the rumbles in high school between the Vaqueros and the Iron Knights; his cousin's arrest; and the crying that seemed to last for days when his grandfather died. Beneath the glide of his thoughts, Wager heard the mumble of Denby's voice; its final phrase and a waiting silence brought him back.

"The warden's secretary said he'd check with some of the guards and call us back."

"Fine. Let's go for a ride."

In the car, Denby finally asked, "Where to?"

Wager eased into the heavy traffic swerving around the gray stone statehouse. "I spotted a car at the Import Shop last night belonging to Francisco Xavier Martinez, 800 Thirtieth Street."

"Last night? What time?"

"About one."

"What in the hell were you doing there at that time of night?"

"I thought I'd swing by after filing Labelle."

"Jesus, don't you ever sleep?"

"Not worth a damn lately."

Denby yawned widely. "Boy, I did! And was it good!"

"I'm glad to hear it."

The neighborhood's large older homes were being cut up into apartments for transients, secretaries, older people, kids going to the new metro university. They all seemed to have cars and bicycles and no place to park them; finally backing into a distant space at the curb, Wager noted Martinez's Buick Skylark across the street from the apartments. The Dalewood's foyer was a tiny box lined with mailboxes and a locked inner door; another door, Apartment 1, was labeled "Manager." Wager verified the name on the mailbox for Apartment 6.

"Want to try it?"

Wager nodded and rang the buzzer. A woman's voice answered through the door, "Manager! Be right there."

The door opened a few inches. "Yes?" She was a short nervous woman with one of those faces that seemed to be pulled to a point by the nose.

"I'm Detective Wager, Denver Police Department. I'd like to ask you a few questions about a tenant."

80

"You got identification?"

"Yes, ma'am."

She peered at the card and badge. "Wager, is it? What can I help you with? My husband isn't here—he's down trying to get a valve for the heating element. It's old and it's always going out and nobody carries the parts any more. But he should be back soon. Who is it you're after?"

"Just some information about one of your tenants, ma'am. Francisco Xavier Martinez, Apartment 6."

"Oh, him. He seems awful nice. I rent to some Mexicans and they seem nice. Mostly quiet and pay their bills. What kind of trouble's he in?"

"There are no warrants on him, ma'am. We'd just like some information about anybody who visits him."

"Visitors? He don't have visitors. Most people here don't have visitors. It's a quiet place."

"Doesn't anybody come see him?" Denby asked.

"Not that I know of. My husband might of seen somebody, but Mr. Martinez don't spend much time around the apartment, and when he does he's pretty quiet. You can't tell if he's in or out most of the time. I guess he spends a lot of time at one of the Mexican restaurants. You're Mexican, ain't you? You know how they do—it's like a club, I guess."

Wager nodded. "Do you know the name of the restaurant?"

"Can't say as I do. There's a half a dozen around here. A lot of Mexicans are moving in, and some of them not so nice. No offense, but you know what I mean."

"Yes, ma'am. Did Martinez sign a lease for the room?"

"Apartment. We don't rent rooms, just apartments. And yes, he did."

"Do you have a copy?"

"Certainly! We don't rent without at least a six-month lease, one month in advance for damage deposit. That's how we keep a good clientele. It's awful easy around here to start renting rooms by the day or week, and first thing you know a nice place is turned into a flophouse. There's a lot of hippies, too, that don't care for nothing and tear a place up in no time. This is a nice apartment house, and me and Mr. Miller aim to keep it that way."

"Yes, ma'am. Can we see a copy of the lease?"

"Certainly. Glad to help out the police. You come when we need you, I reckon we should be here when you need us."

"Yes, ma'am. Thank you."

She held the door for them to come into the living room, a long box with bay windows covered by white curtains spotted with tiny cotton balls. The pigeonhole desk against the wall served as the office and she riffled through a drawer for a few moments. "Here it is. You can't take it with you, but you can look at it. What kind of trouble's Mr. Martinez in?"

"None that we know of, ma'am. It's some of his friends we're worried about."

"Well, he seems like a mighty nice man. And pays his bills. I'm sure if his friends are up to no good, he don't know nothing about it."

"He won't even know we were asking about him if you don't tell him, Ma'am." The form read "Employment: salesman at 1543 W. 38th. Personal reference: Diana Lucero, 3422 Kalamath. Prior address: 764 Navajo, Farmington, New Mexico. Vehicle: 1971 Buick Skylark, Colo. plates BC 7130." Wager finished copying the information. "We'd appreciate it if you kept this confidential, Ma'am. There's no sense upsetting Mr. Martinez for nothing."

"That's so—he's a nice man."

They sat a few moments in Wager's car as he leafed through the notebook. "This Diana Lucero, she lives at the same address as Henry Alvarez."

"And Martinez is a salesman for the Rare Things."

"Which doesn't sell much of anything."

Wager radioed for a make on Diana Lucero and drove down Champa toward the police building. The reply came back when they were two or three blocks from the police center: "No DPD number, no warrants."

"Ten-four." That made it a little harder; he was getting into the vague area where official data left off but the suspect's actions and contacts kept up. It was an area where informants were a must, but with the Alvarez family it would have to be someone from the inside. Cruising through the parking compound, he finally located a slot on the crowded asphalt.

"Let's see if we can find Masters," he said. "Maybe he got to Annie."

They located the Negro detective drinking coffee in the cubicle that was his office. He pulled two more cups off a shelf and wiped them with a paper towel.

"How's Annie?"

"We kept her up all night before we booked her—great God amighty, I'm tired! Cream and sugar?"

"Black."

Denby shook his head. "I had a lot this morning. Too much coffee's bad for the heart."

"Oh?" Masters' wide brown eyes queried Wager, who glanced away.

"Did you get anything?"

"Oh. No. But she's getting ripe. The public defender's with her now. He's gonna show her she ain't got a chance; then I'll lay a deal on her."

"See what she knows about the supplier. Labelle said he was a Chicano kid, but that's all she let slip."

"Hey, we getting integrated pushers! That this Alvarez dude you're after?"

"It could be one of his associates. I don't think it's Alvarez himself. He's no kid."

"I see." The telephone buzzed and Masters said "All right" into the mouthpiece and hung up. "The public defender's leaving. You want to come with me?"

"I'd like to."

"I better stay here," said Denby.

"You better, man! Little Annie's a little pissed at you."

She waited in one of the windowless interrogation rooms, still pulling deeply on the cigarette left by the defender. The matron, a skinny white who looked as if she had sour thoughts about all men, asked, "How long do you want her?"

Masters shrugged. "Half-hour, maybe. We'll call when we're through." He turned the chairback toward Annie and draped himself over it to stare into her worried face. "Hello, missy."

The younger woman grunted and stared dully at Wager through the glare of the lamp, then back to the tabletop greased by sweaty arm prints.

"The public defender's told you we got a case on you," Masters said. "We got your ass, Annie, busted and booked, and we're gonna get a conviction, too. I bet the defender told you to plead guilty and ask for court's mercy. The old first-offense bit.''

"He told me I didn't have to talk to you!"

"He didn't tell you he was gonna get you off, did he?"

"I bet you and him in this together."

"We don't have to be, missy. I *know* when I got a good case. And you are it.''

She sucked the cigarette down to a crackling ash, her forehead pinched into deep wrinkles that made her look far older than her twenty-four years.

"That public defender's right about one thing—he ain't got a defense," Masters said. "But you better listen to me, little mama: there ain't nobody can guarantee you court's mercy.''

"It ain't but a first offense. I ain't never been busted before.''

"It ain't one count, Annie, it's two. And them things add up, first offense or not. And I'll lay something else on you, foxy: you black, and the man, he's white.''

She finished the cigarette and jabbed it against the cardboard ashtray, sending it sliding and spilling off the table.

"Annie, you know where I'm coming from.''

"I know.''

"You know where I'm going, too.''

"I can't do it!"

"There ain't nothing *to* do. All you got to do is make a phone call every now and then. I ain't asking you to buy and I ain't asking you to set anybody up.''

"And you ain't asking me to snitch!"

"I'm giving you a chance to get out of this.'' Masters offered her a cigarette; she stared at it a few moments before she shrugged and reached for it. "Don't make it any harder for me, Annie. It ain't everybody the DA says OK to.''

"What I gotta do?'' she said dully.

"Here's the deal—I go to the DA and ask him to hold up proceedings. What that means is you don't even go to court. If he says yes—and maybe he won't—then your charges go in the drawer.''

"What's that mean?"

"That means we hold on to them and can file them again at any time."

"That DA's gonna own me!"

"No, not him, baby, me," Masters said. "I'm the one that's gonna own you."

"I be better off in jail!"

"We can fix that right quick."

"It ain't fair—it's a first arrest!"

"Ha, where's a nigger gal get treated fair—you tell me that!"

"Well, that lawyer said . . ."

"He said 'chances are,' or 'the court's often lenient,' or 'maybe the judge will appreciate.' That's what he said. You better listen to me, Annie, and listen good because I'm getting short on time. I can maybe get you off if you're willing to give me a call every now and then. If not, then you can take your chances in court with that honky public defender and that honky judge. It's up to you." He shoved the chair back and stood into the dimness above the lamp.

She looked up toward him, the glare of the light etching the lines on her face even deeper; then she stared at Wager. He stared back without blinking and listened to the heavy silence of the room and to the periodic rush of traffic outside.

Her eyes fell from the men and stared again at the table. "All right." Then she looked up angrily. "But I ain't gonna snitch on no friends of mine!"

"Sure, baby. I wouldn't ask you that!" Masters opened the door to call the matron. "We'll know this afternoon if the DA buys it. Hang in there, baby."

"Yeah—ain't no place else to hang."

In the hall, Masters grinned at Wager. "What'd I tell you, man! That old racist shit works every time!"

"I think you got a good one, Charlie."

"Yeah. I bet she's good for a year. Maybe two."

Wager, interrupted by his radio, couldn't answer. "This is two-one-two."

"You have an urgent call at 837-3496."

That was Howie's number; Wager borrowed Masters's phone and dialed an outside line, then the customs agent.

"Hi, Howie, what do you have for me?"

"I've got a no-no."

"What's that mean?"

"It means Juárez would like your cooperation with Valdez."

"They want *my* cooperation? I'm asking them to cooperate with me!"

"He's really a valuable CI, Gabe. You wouldn't believe the stuff he comes up with. Information that nobody else ever had a chance at."

"He may be real deep into heroin in my territory. I just want some information on him. It was his car I spotted."

"His car isn't him. He hasn't been north of El Paso in a month and there's nothing on him locally about any heroin. El Paso port authorities aren't about to stir him up for no reason. You know how it is with a good CI. And Valdez has really come up with some heavy tips."

"What about existing information—known associates, history, records, that stuff?"

"Oh, sure. No problem with that. They're sending it up as soon as they get it together, and I should have it in a few days. They just don't want anybody messing with him unless there's substantial evidence. And they want to be notified of any action concerning him."

"Well, I sure as hell can't move on him in Texas, can I? That's a little beyond my jurisdiction."

"El Paso authorities are just nervous, Gabe. He's number one in their stable, and ninety-five percent reliable, too. You can understand how they feel."

"A good snitch is hard to find."

"If they're like Valdez."

"I'd appreciate a call when the information comes in."

"As soon as I get it."

Masters and Denby looked at him as he set the phone down. "Mexican connection?"

"More like a disconnection," he said.

7

Whenever Wager took time to think about the philosophy of
his business, it seemed to boil down to a handful of familiar
words that probably fit every other business, too: patience,
memory, luck, persistence, detail, sequence. The last wasn't
the most important, but without it none of the detective work
built into a court case; and without a court case the detective
work wasn't worth a feathery fart. Sequence of events, sequence of cause and effect, sequence of evidence, sequence of
testimony. A detective had to be a lawyer, and a sneaky,
crafty, tricky one, if he wasn't to lose the case before it even
got to court. Like the Alvarez file: he could see it all, could
lay out the action with a lot of truth—Rafael at the top, with a
connection in El Paso; lieutenants, brother Henry and
nephew Anthony, and maybe another couple of people who
supervised the bagmen and the drops; Francisco Martinez
one of the bagmen. He could see it, but what he saw would
never get to court without all the little steps of fact and
corroboration. A game. It was all a game where the rules of
play were more important than the right or wrong of an act,
and when you finally sent someone up it was punishment not
for breaking a law but for the defense not playing the game as
well as the prosecution.

Even now, as he sat on the smooth yellow wood of the
courtroom bench and waited for Labelle's plea, the dark-
faced woman sitting in the empty jury box with her warden
seemed no longer to be the person he had arrested, but a
distant object in an impersonal game. The distance used to
bother him; somehow it seemed that the prisoner should be
striding nervously back and forth from the bench to the table
to the jury box. The prisoner always seemed aloof from his
own trial, as if he weren't really there to be tried, weren't
really there to be punished. It had bothered him until finally

he realized that he was just as distant, that he—the arresting officer—was also an object in a game whose players stroke back and forth with their hint of self-conscious drama or sat murmuring together at the bleak tables on each side of the arena. Labelle sat and watched; he sat and watched. They would be called and used as testimony and then dismissed, and the game would play to its end while they watched.

Wager stood at the bailiff's cry as Judge McCormick entered to start the afternoon session. Then came the usual settling-down noises, the shuffle of papers by the judge, the relaxing and shifting by the spectators and witnesses scattered over the rows of long polished benches, the fading murmur from lawyers allowed to use the tiny chambers as a waiting room. The judge checked the docket and mumbled a few words to the stenographer, who mumbled a reply; at last he nodded to the bailiff.

"The City and County of Denver against Labelle Browne: charges, illegal possession of narcotics, illegal possession of narcotics with intent to sell, illegal possession of a dangerous firearm. . . ."

Labelle, ushered from the jury box to stand before the high paneled wall of the judge's bench, looked small between the bailiff and the public defender. The judge droned the penalties in a voice just loud enough to be heard by Wager; then he asked for the plea. The defender answered for her. The judge leaned forward a little to look directly down at the woman. "Do you understand the consequences of your plea?"

"She does, Your Honor."

"Let her answer for herself, counselor. Do you understand the consequences of your plea?"

"Yeah, Judge, I do."

"Knowing the consequences of your plea, do you persist in it?"

Labelle was silent until the defender smiled and asked, "Would you please rephrase the question, Your Honor?"

"I suppose I'd better. Miss Browne, if you plead guilty, you know you're going to jail, and you might go for as long as fifteen years. Do you still want to plead guilty?"

"Yas, suh, Your Honor."

"All right—record the plea. Any character witnesses or

special circumstances you wish to bring forth at this time?"

"Not at this time, sir."

"Is the arresting officer present?"

Wager stood. "Here, sir."

"Would you approach the bench, please?"

He stood at the base of the oak panels and gazed up at the judge, who seemed miles beyond. Strange, even after so many times spent looking over that distance to a judge's face, the gap still seemed as far.

"Unless counsel has objection, I'd like to ask the arresting officer about the defendant's behavior at time of arrest." Judge McCormick had some psychological theory about behavior at time of arrest that no one had ever figured out. But the DA's office told Wager to be here to answer the judge's questions, and here he stood.

"No objections, Your Honor."

"Let the record so state. Well, Detective Wager, how did the defendant behave?"

He glanced at Labelle, who stood, eyes down, collecting all emotion in tense fists at her sides. "She didn't resist arrest, Your Honor."

"And has she been cooperative since?"

"No, sir."

"I see." He leafed through the pages of Labelle's file and glanced up. "Thank you, Detective Wager, that's all."

"Yes, sir." Wager pushed through the low gate into the spectator's area and to his seat. The judge, after a few moments of consulting his calendar, set sentencing for two weeks away, tapped his gavel, and Labelle was hustled off by the warden. The bailiff was charged to call the next name; Wager left as prosecution and defense closed the old file and shuffled the new one in preparation for another case.

In the echoing hall outside the courtroom, Wager paused to read through his notebook on Alvarez, hunting for dangling threads. It was time to lean on Leonard; things had been too slow and that little bastard should have something by now. And the New Mexico and El Reno authorities had to be called again, and maybe El Paso had stopped stalling and sent the file up on Valdez. Francisco X. Martinez. Diana Lucero. More names, more threads. And Masters—maybe Masters finally got something from Annie about her supplier. Most of it could be done by phone, and then he'd better start cruising.

At his desk, he picked up the phone and began with Masters. The MEG detective answered with his official voice.

"This is Gabe, Charlie. Did Annie give you anything on her supplier?"

"Naw. She still claims she doesn't know the dude. But she did come up with an address where they picked the stuff up."

"Are you going to come down on it?"

"If I ever get the goddam time, man. I'm supposed to be working up in Boulder again this week. You want to run a raid on this address?"

"Will Annie talk to me about it first?"

"Why?"

"Because I can't raid anybody unless you go along or unless she tells me personally. It's an extension of the double-hearsay rule."

"Shit! Well, Annie's not about to open up to anyone else, and I'm hauling my ass up to Boulder as soon as I can."

"Give me the number anyway. I'd like to eyeball the place."

"Right. Hang on." The receiver clattered onto the desk top and Wager waited a few moments. Suzy brought him a fresh pot of coffee and he nodded thanks. "Here it is, 1712 Clarkson. Basement apartment, no number."

He repeated the address. "By the way, tell Annie that her girl friend will probably get eight to ten."

Masters whistled into the phone. "That's more than I thought she'd get. Who was the judge?"

"McCormick."

"He don't take no shit. He ask you if she'd cooperated?"

"Yeah. I had to say no."

"Right on, brother! That's one less piece of shit floating around."

"You know it."

"Be cool, brother."

His next call was to Farmington, New Mexico; the WATS operator said she would call back when the line was clear. He fiddled briefly with the coffee, then dialed Leonard's number. It rang twelve or fifteen times before he hung up.

Leonard was probably listening to it ring, probably guessed who it was, and was sitting there with that sick little sneer that passed for a smile. Wager would have to go by and drag him out of his hole and come down on him. Which really wasn't unpleasant: he knew exactly what snarls and whines would be squeezed out, and he had to admit to satisfaction in watching his own games play out the way he knew they would.

The phone rang and Suzy answered it; Wager, waiting for the Farmington call, grabbed the receiver when she nodded. But it wasn't New Mexico—a twangy Texas voice answered Wager's hello: "This here's Assistant Warden John Short from El Reno. I got you a little information on the Alvarez brothers."

"Fine." .

The voice drawled through the federal prison numbers, dates of incarceration, and rehabilitation reports, then came to what Wager was listening for: "We don't have much on their associates while in prison, but here's their cellmates: Felix (none) Martinez, aka Happy, number 2317652; possession and manslaughter; residence at time of arrest, El Paso, Texas; currently in El Reno prison. Pedro Gonzales Moreno, aka Pete Mitchell, number 2329745; possession and selling; residence at time of arrest, El Paso, Texas; paroled 23 December 1971. Edward David Hart, aka Eddie, number 2319649; possession and transporting; residence at time of arrest, Fabens, Texas; paroled 26 June 1973."

"Where's Fabens, Texas?"

"A little town just east of El Paso—more dogs than people, and more fleas than dogs." Short read two or three more names, and Wager recorded them and thanked him. Then he stared out the window as the names collected around what he knew and what he guessed. Eddie Hart, the source of the Seattle tip; that explained why Hart didn't have his facts straight—he just heard cell talk. Three addresses in or near El Paso; that would be the Mexican connection. He called customs again and asked for Agent Hartnoll.

"Howie, have you ever heard of Edward David Hart, or Felix Martinez, aka Happy, or Pedro Gonzales Moreno, aka Pete Mitchell? They're from the El Paso area."

"Moreno—I was in on his bust. Felix was sent up before I

got there. I never ran across Hart."

"They were the Alvarez brothers' cellmates in El Reno."

A few seconds of silence. "That's the link to Fuzzy Valdez, then."

"How's that?"

"Fuzzy tipped us off on Moreno. They're cousins by marriage or something."

"Valdez snitched on his own cousin?"

"Moreno'll never know. Hell, he wouldn't believe it now if you told him. We did a good job covering Fuzzy. In fact, Fuzzy and Moreno own a tourist shop together in Juárez"—Hartnoll laughed—"Fuzzy used the snitch money to buy the shop, and brought Moreno in when he got out of prison. Moreno thinks Fuzzy's God."

"His own cousin!"

"That's what I mean about Fuzzy; we don't want to lose anybody who'd snitch on his own cousin."

"I wonder if we could work something out on Valdez."

"Not without the El Paso authorities' OK. And you won't get that unless you've got a hell of a lot more evidence than a possibly borrowed car."

"And I can't get the evidence without the OK."

"If you do get something more, I'll help you as much as I can."

"What about the file on Valdez that I asked for?"

"All I can tell you is what they tell me—they're working on it."

"Yeah. Thanks, Howie."

Wager scraped the pencil on his notebook and started another cup of coffee, cut it in half with powdered milk as he felt the case begin to pile up like acid in his stomach—the familiar impatient feeling that came when things were beginning to click but not yet fast enough; when, with a little help or a small break, he could nail together a coffin-tight case that even the DA's office couldn't blow. But the break didn't come; the help wasn't offered. "Suzy, is Denby going to be in today?"

"He's in court in Boulder on that Louisville bust a couple of months ago."

"The one where he chased the guys down?"

She nodded. "He didn't think it would take too long."

But it would be too long; Wager knocked on Sergeant Johnston's doorframe. "Ed, we're starting to get somewhere on the Alvarez case." He told the sergeant about the call from El Reno and his talk with Hartnoll. "I'd like to have some help from DEA—we're getting out of our jurisdiction."

The lanky sergeant unfolded awkwardly from behind his desk and rubbed the thin fuzz on his head. "They do owe us, and it looks like an interstate thing. Let me give a call over there. Maybe somebody's free now."

Wager waited while Johnston went through his old-friend routine with the sergeant at the other end of the line. After questions about the wife, health, budget, weather, cost of living, unionization, old friends long departed and some just found, restaurants, and the energy shortage, Johnston finally asked his favor. "That's fine, George; Billy's a good man— he used to be with us. Right. Right. He'll be working with Wager again. Right. We're all in it together. Right. Real fine, George, and thanks again." He turned, smiling, to Wager who did his best to look patient. "Wow, that guy likes to talk! But it's OK, Gabe. Billington's in court in Boulder right now, but as soon as he's through he's joining us."

"Is that the case Denby's on?" Knowing damn well that they both knew damn well.

"I do believe it is."

"How long's that supposed to last?"

"George didn't say. It shouldn't be too long, though. Straight buy and bust, I believe."

"It's the one where Denby chased down the suspects and searched their car. It was not a guilty plea. The admissible evidence is going to be pretty thin. It will probably last a week or more."

Johnston's smile slowly went away. "Look, Wager, if this Alvarez is as big as you think he is, he'll stay around for a while—he's not going anyplace. And your cases aren't the only ones in this unit. If you get the hots to get something done, get off your ass and do it. Billington and Denby will be available when they're available and not before. You understand?"

He understood. Wager went back to his desk and stood a few quivering moments to let the anger hiss away in slow breaths: a goddamned desk sergeant telling him to get off his

93

ass! He jammed his radiopack in its holster. "Suzy, I'm waiting for a WATS call for Farmington. When it comes through, ask them about Francisco Xavier Martinez, last address 764 Navajo—about six months to a year ago. I want copies of any records they have on him." He wrote the name on a memo sheet for her. "I'll be on the street if anybody wants me."

Leonard's address was one of those small brick hotels that never seem to have any business and whose special weekly rates—paid in advance—let it survive on a relatively stable list of lodgers. The dimly lit hallway smelled of dusty steam heat and faint urine, and Wager, as he stood by Leonard's door and listened, half wondered if the residents ever got used to it. A faint creak came under the door and he knew Leonard waited against the other side, listening for Wager's footsteps to fade down the worn carpet. Wager spoke just loudly enough to be heard through the peeling wood, "Hello, Leonardo. You're there and I'm here. Open up."

The silence behind the door was thicker than an empty room could be. Wager felt his own presence pushing against the dark door and knew that Leonard felt it, too. "Open up, you little bastard, or I'll give you a lesson in police brutality."

Another tiny creak, then the gritty scrape of a bolt and lock; the door opened just wide enough for one of Leonard's brown eyes to peer at Wager. "Oh, it's you." He opened it quickly and peeked up and down the hall before locking it behind them.

"What's this game?" Wager asked.

"It's all your fault—you set me up and made me ask questions. Now they think I was the one that unloaded the heroin snitch."

"Who's they?" Wager's eyes adjusted to the gloom of the curtained window; the urine smell was stronger, mingled with a sourness of filthy bedding, old grease, and some ripeness he couldn't quite identify. He shoved aside a curtain and heaved at the paint-encrusted window.

"What the fuck you doing?"

"Letting in some air. This place smells like a whorehouse crapper on Sunday morning."

"Well it ain't my fault. I been too scared to even go down

94

the hall and take a shit!''

So instead he used the sink in the corner. Wager fought down a surge of vomit and stood at the window to breathe. ''Who's they?''

''You know who—the Alvarez family.''

''Give me the story.''

''You told me to get some information on him, so I asked around.'' He opened a drawer in the wobbly dresser and pulled out a bottle. ''I should have told you to shove it up your ass. I shouldn't of let you make me do it. Now look what you got me into.'' He waved his fist at Wager and held the whiskey bottle up for two, three large gulps. ''Jesus, my stomach! I gotta get some protection. Wager, you gotta get me some protection. You got me into this shit, now you gotta get me out.''

''What the hell happened?''

''I'm telling you! I was asking around about Alvarez like you made me do, and this friend of mine comes up and says I better split—that one of Alvarez's cousins or nephews or something heard I was finking on them for you and he was going to waste me.''

''You don't have friends. Who told you?''

''I got friends! I got friends, Wager, and you ain't one of them!''

''Scum like you doesn't have friends. You've got people who know you and people who don't. That's all. Now, who gave you the word to split?''

''You son of a bitch, I got friends!''

Wager grinned and waggled a finger at the dim figure. ''Come here and look out the window, Leonardo. The sun's shining, the sky's blue, there's people walking up and down without a worry in the world. Cars, bicycles, buses, taxis, everybody has someplace to go. Except you. You have no place and nobody, Leonard. Come on—come on over and look outside. And see how many friends you've got; see how many people say 'Hi, Leonard,' and see if that sky gets any bluer because you're looking at it.''

The figure held the bottle and didn't move from the shadow between the bureau and the unmade bed. ''Wager, I hate your guts.''

Still grinning, Wager pushed open another curtain. ''Let's

95

have some people see you. Come on over here, if you think you've got friends. Come on!''

Leonard shook his head rapidly. ''Close the curtains, you dumb son of a bitch!''

He pushed them further open. ''Who gave you the word?''

''Close the curtains, Wager!''

''Who was it?''

''You son of a bitch, it was Frankie Martinez!''

He closed one set of curtains and went back to the open window to breathe. ''Francisco Xavier Martinez—from Farmington?''

''He used to live there, yeah.'' Leonard pulled again at the bottle and coughed deeply.

''Why'd he tip you?''

''He owed me one.''

''For what? What the hell did you ever do for anybody?''

''Leave me alone!'' The wail rose and fell into a nasal whine and Leonard thumped the whiskey bottle on the gritty bureau top.

''Why'd he owe you?''

''We did time in Santa Fe together. We were . . . friends.''

''So that's what you mean when you say you've got friends! Well, I'll be damned, Leonardo-baby!''

''I'm straight now, you bastard. You don't know what it's like in that place. If you don't have friends, you get used. You gotta have a friend so you can look after each other.''

''Sure, Leonard, and you're such a nice piece. How did Frankie-baby find out about the hit sign?''

Leonard mumbled, ''He's part of the family. He's a second cousin or something.''

''You two still ass-hole buddies?''

''No! I told you, goddam it, I been straight since I got out!''

''How long's Frankie been working for Alvarez?''

''I don't know. A few months, maybe. I didn't even know he was in town until I saw him on the street.''

''That must have been a sweet surprise.''

Even in the dimness, Leonard's eyes glittered with wet rage. ''Fuck you, Wager!''

''You're not my type, sweetie.'' He counted out fifty dollars and waved the bills at the rigid figure. ''Here, shitbird, here's some of the taxpayers' money. Now you listen: I'm going to talk to Frankie-baby and I'm going to tell him I got the word from you. If you've got any smarts left in that screwed-up skull of yours, you'll get out of town right now, if not sooner."

"Don't do it, Wager—they'll be after me for sure! Fifty bucks ain't enough to run nowhere!"

"It's all you're worth."

"I been tipping you! I been giving you information for two years—don't do it to me." He lunged forward, knocking the bottle over, and grabbed Wager's coat.

The raw whiskey smell spread over the stench of the room as Wager pushed the dumpy body back into the widening puddle. "I have to work too hard to get information out of you, Leonardo. I'm getting too old to work so hard; I got to think of my health. Now, I'm giving you a chance to skip before I talk to Martinez. I should just let Alvarez scrub you—you're a wart, a walking insult to Hispanos. Get the fuck off me before I call Alvarez myself."

"Don't do it, Wager. For God's sake don't. I'll work for you! I'll really work. I'll call you every week, really! I'll get good stuff for you!"

"I've heard it before."

"I mean it, goddam it! Don't tell Frankie—if he knows I told you, he'll come after me himself!"

He was tempted; Leonard still had some usefulness and Wager had found another lever to squeeze him with. But alive he was no good for getting to Alvarez—and no good dead for getting to Frankie. Best if he just disappeared. "All right, you slimy wad of shit, come on."

"Where to?"

"Out of town."

"I don't want to leave. Just give me a place to hole up in until it's over."

"If Alvarez didn't find you first, you'd asphyxiate yourself. And right now you're worth more alive than dead."

"Come on, Wager. I live here—I don't know anyplace else!"

"The world is waiting for your entrance."

"I gotta have money, Wager. You owe me. . . ."

"I owe you zilch, *amigo*. But I'll do this much just to get

97

rid of you: a free one-way ticket and a little extra sugar. That's all. Now, if you want the deal, come on. Right now, and leave all this crap here—I don't want anybody to know you're not coming back. Or else stay here and be wasted."

"Wait a minute, I'm coming!" He fumbled for two or three things in the back of his dresser and jammed them into the grime-rimmed pockets of his coat, then yanked it on and stumbled after Wager, who was already at the stairwell. "Wait, goddam it—you gotta stay close to me!"

At his office, Wager set Leonard on a chair next to the open window and went in to see Johnston.

"How far do you want to send him?"

Wager shrugged. "Far enough so he'll stay alive for a few months."

"LA? New York? Texas?"

"New York. Alvarez probably won't have connections there."

"Gotham City it is." The sergeant filled out a chit and called the bus depot for the fare and time. He scribbled in the amount and added a hundred for expenses, then counted out the cash as Wager initialed the receipt.

"Come on Leonard, you've got twenty minutes."

Wager drove him to the bus depot and ushered him through the small lobby to the ticket window.

"Where the shit are you sending me?"

"New York. It's an express bus and makes eight stops, and I'm calling ahead to make sure you stay on the bus. If you get off between here and New York, I'll know when and where, and I'll make that phone call to Alvarez."

"Hey, I don't want to go to New York!"

Wager bought the ticket and then clamped his hand around Leonard's arm hard enough to make him wince. "Don't give me any more crap. I'm putting you on that bus. Then I'm going to lean on your boyfriend. Here"—he stuffed the roll of bills in Leonard's coat pocket—"it's more than you ever earned."

Leonard seemed to lose air, shriveling up inside the grimy suit that was too big to start with, until he looked half the size he was. "Wager, I don't want to go. I don't even know anybody there. I'm gonna die there, I know it."

"You're dead if you stay here, and I don't want your carcass in my territory."

98

Leonard stared at Wager and started to speak. Then stopped. Then blurted, "I used to think maybe it was almost a game between you and me. You know, we bad-mouth each other and then you say you're not going to give me any break and I say I'm not going to give you any information, and we both know we'll deal in the end. It was a kind of game." He paused and picked with dirty fingernails at a thread on his cuff. "Christ, Wager, I don't know nobody in New York. Please don't send me there."

"There's the bus. It's loading now."

"It never was a game with you, was it? I mean the way it was for me?"

Wager said nothing; he pulled the man after him toward the open door of the bus where a gray-uniformed driver stood checking tickets and helping an old lady reach the first step.

"Wager, of all the people I know, and I know some bad dudes, you're the worst. You are a real bastard."

"You want a kiss good-bye, Leonardo-baby?"

The brown suit bunched through the doorway in silence. Wager stood in the shadow of the concrete awning and surveyed the boarding passengers following Leonard on. They all looked straight; he recognized none of them. Leonard, an invisible shape behind the tinted windows, stayed on the bus. The driver finally locked the luggage compartment and climbed to his seat, then pumped the metal door shut and cranked the engine into a cloud of black smoke. A few moments later, the bus was around the corner and lost in late-afternoon traffic.

In his car, Wager radioed to Suzy, "Any word from New Mexico yet on Martinez?"

8

It took two more days before Wager could get out to the Clarkson address where Labelle had her meet. It was a one-way street jammed with two lanes of cars squeezing past bumper-to-bumper parking; at this end, tunneling beneath diseased elms soon to be stripped and burned, it led uphill toward the capitol building. Some of the big, old houses were still private residences, some had apartment-to-rent signs— all were a comfortable distance back from the traffic. Wager, as he walked across the lawn to the screen door of 1712, felt the tension sag from his shoulders in the same way that the buildings themselves showed a comfortable sagging line here and there. It was nice to find an area that lacked the raw rigidity of so many of the newer parts of Denver—an area that had trees big enough to shade the second story, that had large deep screened porches wrapped around the old-fashioned square windows, that had peeling white garages distant from the house across broad back yards, with here and there a tire swinging gently beneath a thick limb. It was the kind of neighborhood he had sneaked into as a boy and wished he could live in, a neighborhood that, despite the traffic and threat of blight, still breathed space and comfort and order.

On the surface.

But beneath—under the bark of the elm trees, in the shadows of the porches, behind the curtained windows, in the basement apartments crammed with five and sometimes ten runaway kids camping in filth, in the night's blackness that filled the alleys and creaking empty garages—lay what brought him here now. And the tension began to come back as he pressed the button in the center of the rusting metal flower surrounding the doorbell.

A small Chicano opened the door and stared silently at him.

"Is your mama home, son?"

The wide black eyes peered a moment more; then the boy wheeled from the door and screamed, "Mama!" A moment or two later, his mother came: mid-twenties, beginning to spread from children and starchy diet, early prettiness already fading beneath the suspicion that was becoming a permanent frown on her face.

Wager showed his identification. "I'm running a state security check on a person who gave this address as a former place of residence. Would you mind answering a question or two about him?"

"Do I have to?"

Wager paused for effect. "Not right now, Ma'am. But if we subpoena you we'll have to ask you to appear in court. That'll take more time."

"Oh. Well, I'm busy enough as it is. What you want to know?"

"Can I have your name, please?"

"Lucille Trujillo. Who you looking for?"

"I'm not looking for anyone, Mrs. Trujillo; it's a state security check on an applicant for a sensitive position. How long have you lived here, please?"

"Since 1969. What's the name of the guy you're after?"

"Raymond Billington." Billy wouldn't mind if he didn't find out. "Did he live at this residence in 1967?"

"How do I know? I just told you we came here in 1969. The people who we bought it from were named Parker. They lived here a long time. I don't know this Billington."

"Maybe he rented an apartment?"

She shrugged. "They told us they didn't rent. That's why they moved: too many people were renting and a lot of transients were coming in." She grinned. "Like us."

Wager smiled back. "Do you rent apartments?"

"Sure—we got one in the basement. We can't afford not to."

"Can you give me the renter's name? Maybe he knew Mr. Billington."

"John Quintero." She shrugged again. "He won't know this Billington—he only moved in nine months ago."

"Is he home now?"

"Asleep, probably. He works nights at a parking garage

downtown somewhere. Sometimes we don't see him for a week. He has his own door on the side."

"Does he live alone?"

"Yes."

"Does he have many visitors?"

The frown of suspicion came back again. "Who you after, this sensitive guy or Quintero?"

"I'm supposed to find out as much as I can, ma'am."

"Well, he has some visitors every week or so, that's all. We don't see much of him except when he pays the rent. Most of the time, you'd never know he was there. Like I say, he works nights."

"When is his rent due again?"

"Today—first of the month. Listen, anything else you want to know about Mr. Quintero, you ask him. I never heard of this other guy."

"Yes, ma'am. Thank you very much."

He drove a couple of blocks away before calling for a check on the name; by the time he reached the office parking lot, the reply came back: "We have seven John Quinteros or Juan Quinteros, but none at that address. You have a description of the suspect?"

"No, just the name."

"That doesn't help much. You want all this material?"

"No. Thanks anyway." He should have guessed—it was probably a false name anyhow. And now he had one more place to keep an eye on, when he was spread so thin already.

Suzy looked up when he came in. "I've been waiting for you—New Mexico came through with a make on Francisco Xavier Martinez. He did eighteen months in Santa Fe on a vacated suspension—possession of narcotics."

"Why was it vacated?"

"Second conviction of possession. Marijuana."

"Any prison reports on him?"

"None that Farmington had. They said he had time off for good behavior, so there's probably not much."

"Right, good going. Anything from Denby yet?"

"No. I thought he'd be back yesterday afternoon, but he's still up in Boulder."

Wager nodded his disgust and sat down to begin an

103

affidavit for phone taps on the Alvarez residence and place of business. Chances were against getting them: the alternative means of surveillance had not been thoroughly exhausted, and there was only circumstantial evidence of a crime in progress. A lot would depend on which judge it went to. Still, it wouldn't hurt to get started on the preliminary. He began with the first blank in the lines of ritual phrases: "I, <u>Gabriel Wager</u>, being first duly sworn, upon oath depose and state as follows: That I am presently a <u>detective</u> assigned to the <u>Special Narcotics Section</u> of the Denver Police Department, Denver, Colorado, and that in the course of my duties I have obtained information concerning . . ." The first section dealt with information obtained from informants, and he did not have much for that. The second listed the results of surveillance, and there wasn't much there either. The third section was the result of routine investigative procedures—Jesus, he almost let that one slip by! "Suzy, make out a *duces tecum* to Mountain Bell Telephone Company for records on—" he looked up the Rare Things' number and Alvarez's home— "632-6081 and 724-0553. Have them signed as soon as they're done." Other routine investigative procedures . . . He was combing through the pages of the Alvarez journal, trying to pump a little more significance into the evidence, when Denby came in looking subdued.

"Don't tell me—let me guess: you lost them."

"Got a cup of coffee, Suzy?"

"You lost them because the evidence was inadmissible."

"Thanks, Suzy." He blew across the steaming black liquid, which he held under his baggy eyes. "I think I'm getting allergic to coffee."

"Or else the most you could get them on was possession. If the guys ran from you, they didn't intend to sell it."

"Possession. First conviction. Suspended sentence. What a shitty waste!"

"So they're back on the street and dealing right now."

"I guess so. Who the hell cares?"

"OK, so we win a few and lose a lot. Don't waste time crying. I've got the go-ahead on Alvarez, and Johnston says you're to work with me on him."

Denby sipped the coffee and breathed heavily before

shaking himself like a tired fighter. "We might win a few. Sometime. I can't get very excited about anything right now."

Wager ignored Denby's slump and told him about Leonard, Martinez, and the Clarkson Street address.

"Do you want me to deal with Martinez?"

"I better work on him. I'd like you to keep an eye on the Clarkson address—this Quintero's due to pay his rent today. No busts, just surveillance. And swing by this location, too." He wrote down the Kalamath Street number of Henry Alvarez and Diana Lucero. "Oh, yeah, in your spare time I want you to check Ma Bell's records for a couple of numbers. Suzy's finishing up a *duces tecum* subpoena now."

"Jesus. Anything else?"

"I'll see what I can think of. Did Billington come down from Boulder with you?"

"I dropped him at his office."

Wager dialed the DEA agent's number; the secretary called him to the phone. "I wondered how soon you'd call," he said. "Denby told you we blew it?"

"He didn't have to—I knew you would when I heard about the arrest procedure. I don't know why you even took them to court."

"Yeah. Well. Crap. Well, what's this you've got me on now?"

"Alvarez—do you remember him? He's big in heroin now."

"I know the name, but I never had anything to do with him."

"Want to meet him?"

"Why not? I got an interest in criminal types; I want to write a detective story."

"You better learn how to read first. I'll be by your place in a few minutes."

It was like the old times when Billy was his partner. It made Wager feel good to know he'd be working with him again, and Denby must have seen it; his face shifted from gloom to sullenness as he listened. Wager almost smiled at him. "I'm showing Billy the territory; I'll check with you later tonight."

"How long do you want me on these addresses?"

"You have something planned?"

"There's this movie the wife wanted to see. . . ."

"I'll meet you on Clarkson Street about six."

"Right."

Billington was quiet on the way to the Rare Things, the only reference to the lost case being a terse "Crap" when Wager asked about it. Wager sketched in the new case for the DEA agent as he pulled into a parking place down the block from the store. Billington studied the concrete front. "That it? Seems pretty quiet."

"His customers are mostly at night. Late."

"Cash and carry?"

"Cash, anyway. The carry's probably somewhere else. Want to do some shopping?"

"I'm with you."

The bell jingled as they entered the showroom, which was crowded with the same decorations and souvenirs and coated with a film of old dust. Even the air in the room felt slightly stale. The nephew, Anthony, came through the bead curtain from the back room. He slowed to a stop as he recognized Wager, and his eyes went darker with caution and anger.

"Hello, Anthony. Is Uncle Rafael around?"

"No."

"When'll he be back?"

"I don't know." Anthony lit a cigarette, and the flame threw a glow onto his guarded face.

"Where is he?" Wager pushed past the stiff youth to open the bead curtain. The office, empty, still had the feeling of being a well-used living room in a not too well-kept home.

"I told you he ain't here, Wager."

"Did I say I didn't believe you? Where is he?"

"Out of town. On business."

"This is Detective Billington. He's from the Drug Enforcement Agency. He wants to know where Rafael is, too."

A mixture of fright and defiance crossed Anthony's face for a second. "He's still out of town."

"Where out of town?"

"None of your goddamned business, *vendido!*"

"Watch your manners, young man. Your uncle would be disappointed to hear his sister's boy use such language."

Anthony took a final puff on the cigarette and stubbed it out in an ashtray. "What you want with him? You got a warrant on him?"

"We just came to talk to him. When's he coming back?"

"I don't know. I really do not know. I will be very happy to tell him you and your friend came to call."

"Good boy, Anthony! Much better—*muy sofisticado.*" He glanced at the rows of souvenirs in the glass case; they stood unchanged from the last visit. In fact, nothing seemed changed, except that the TV set glowed a football game instead of a baseball game. "How's the mail-order business?"

"Business is real good."

"That's what we hear."

Anthony reached for another cigarette and hid his face in the busy work of taking it out of the package, tapping in the tobacco, lighting it, feeling the smoke in his lungs.

"You tell Rafael I was by, nephew. We'll be seeing you again."

"Yeah. Not if I see you first."

He watched them through the glass panel of the door; Wager smiled good-bye as they walked past the display window and down the block to their car.

"You haven't changed much, Gabe."

"How's that?"

"Whenever you smile at somebody, I feel sorry for them."

"Humor's a personal thing."

"I reckon. What's a *vendido?*"

"Sellout—a turncoat. Little Anthony's the kind who thinks all Chicanos are on one side of the street and all cops are on the other."

"He didn't look so little to me."

"I'm not talking about his size. I'm talking about his manhood. He has a lot to learn."

"He seems to be learning pretty fast."

"I hope he learns self-control as well as his uncle's business."

107

"One of those?"

"One of those. We were close to playing fun and games, just then."

"I wouldn't mind coming down on the son of a bitch any time he wants to try something." Billington whistled shortly between his teeth in the tuneless way that told Wager his mind was attacking, one by one, each fact of the new case. "You say customs hasn't come through on this dude from El Paso—what's his name?"

"Fuzzy Valdez."

"Valdez, Fuzzy. A rat's nest of family and friends. We've got to get to someone inside; the phone tap's not going to be approved unless we have something solid first." He whistled again. "Hell, you've thought of all that already. What have you come up with?"

Since he had put Leonard on the bus, Wager had been thinking of Francisco Martinez; he told Billy about the new suspect. Billy grinned in admiration. "Same old cool Gabe!"

They drove past the store and swung back through the alley. The Mach-1 sat nosed to the concrete block; the rest of the parking lot was empty. "That's Anthony's car." Billington jotted the description down in his notebook; Wager leafed through his until he came to the page of vehicle identifications. "Here's what else I've got on cars and licenses."

Billy copied that, too. "Yeah, I think Martinez might do. Let's drop by my office on the way."

Wager glanced at his watch. "I guess we have time."

"What's the rush?"

"Denby's staked out on Clarkson Street. I told him I'd relieve him at six."

"He only works a forty-hour week?"

Wager tried to keep the embarrassment out of his voice. "His wife wants to go see a movie."

"Jesus H. Christ—it ain't the old corps!"

They inched through the quitting-time traffic that flooded the freeways and the crosstown boulevards. Billington ran into his office and popped back out a few minutes later. "Had to borrow some evidence." Finally, Wager turned out of the stop-and-go lines of cars on Colfax and began looking for a parking place.

108

"How do the TV cops always find a parking place right in front?" Billington said.

"They bribe the meter maid."

"Watch that language, man. The persons in blue are incorruptible."

"Tell that to the Staff Inspection Bureau," Wager said.

"You goddam greasers are a cynical lot."

"It comes from centuries of shameless exploitation by Anglos—rootless immigrants to the land of Aztlan. No colorful culture, no historical past, no cheerful pottery; just money, money, money. No wonder all you Anglos are so rich."

"Yeah. And I eat head lettuce and grapes, too."

Wager punched at Billington's shoulder. "Come on, you blue-eyed son of a bitch, let's go roust a Chicano." It was good to be working with Billy again.

They stood in the small foyer of the Dalewood Apartments and studied the mailboxes. "We're locked out. You want to ring the manager?"

Wager shook his head. "Let's try something quieter." He pressed the button to Apartment 24: "R. Targ." A woman's voice answered, "Who is it?"

"A package for Mrs. R. Targ. It has to be signed for."

"For me?"

"Yes, Ma'am. It has to be signed for."

"Just a minute."

A buzzer clattered as R. Targ cleared the lock on the hallway door. Wager and Billington opened it and the buzzer stopped.

"You lied to that nice lady, Gabe."

"I'll clear my soul at confession."

"You snappers take the easy way out."

"If it wasn't for you black prods, we wouldn't need a hell."

"Is it true all your priests are Irish?"

"Not any more, honky. You've been watching too much Bing Crosby on the *Late Show*."

They stopped at Apartment 6. From inside came the blurred mechanical voice of a television reporter repeating the word "Watergate." Wager knocked on the door; the voice shut off. He knocked again. "Mr. Martinez?"

A few moments of tense movement, stealthy footsteps back and forth across the boards of the old floor.

"He's hiding his stash," muttered Billy. Wager nodded and rapped again.

"Who is it?"

"Police officers, Mr. Martinez. I'd like to ask you some questions about Leonard Solano."

Quicker footsteps on the floor; Wager rapped harder. "He's been shot. I'd like to ask you some questions."

"All right, all right!" The door lock clicked and a chain and bolt rattled. Martinez stood in the half-open door scowling; he was slightly shorter than Wager, had the usual dark hair and eyes, and a round face with a Cantinflas mustache, shaved in the middle of the upper lip and heavy at the corners of his mouth. He was in his late twenties. "Who's this you want to ask me about?"

Wager showed his identification and pushed into the room; Billy closed the door and, as Wager talked Martinez back into the middle of the small living room, went through the apartment in a restless search. "Don't shit me, Frankie; you did time with Leonard in New Mexico. He's one of my Concerned Individuals."

"Your what?"

"CIs—snitches. Leonard's in my stable. He said you told him somebody was going to waste him."

"No! I never told nobody nothing like that!" Martinez sank onto the spindly-legged couch facing the color set.

Wager propped a foot on the smooth plastic of the couch and leaned over the man's paling face. "I'm not in the mood for your kind of cheap crap, Martinez. You and Leonard were kissing cousins, you goddamned pervert, and you tipped him that Alvarez was going to smoke him. You work for Alvarez now, and if you know what's good for you, you'll work for me. I want information on Alvarez's setup."

"No, man! Hell, no, man!" He lunged up from the couch; Wager jabbed his fingertips into Martinez's throat and bounced him back. "That hurt!" he said, gasping for air.

"I'm real good at hurting people, Frankie-baby. Now you better hear me good. I've got Leonard hidden away in protective custody. Alvarez's people are going to want to know why he disappeared and who tipped him. They're going to
110

remember that you two were ass-hole buddies.''

"You said somebody offed him!"

"I lied to you, Frankie. So you'd open the door, Frankie. Right now you're in shit up to your eyes, Frankie. All I have to do is whisper, and under you go.''

"You're lying now. Lenny wouldn't fink on me!"

"Lenny would. And did. He got his tail out of a crack and put yours in.''

"That ain't true!"

Wager grinned into the man's eyes. "Give Anthony a call and ask him if anybody tried to hit Leonard. He's at the Rare Things.''

"No . . .''

Wager pulled the directory from under the small Danish Modern table at the end of the couch where the telephone sat. "I'll call. I'll tell Anthony you were just curious.''

"Jesus, no!"

Wager looked up the number and lifted the receiver. "If you think I'm lying, give him a call.'' He poked the first four numbers on the lit buttons. "You want to talk to him or do you want me to?''

"Give it here!" He poked the last numbers and glared at Wager as it rang. "Anthony? This is Frankie. Say, listen, I—uh—heard that somebody got to Leonard Solano. No, I don't know. I thought maybe you knew. No! I ain't seen him since Santa Fe—you know that! I just heard it on the street is all. I don't know. Sure, Anthony, whatever you say. *Por supuesto*. Yeah. I'll try to find out. Sure, Anthony. OK. Good-bye.'' He set the phone on the cradle and stared blankly at Wager. "He don't know nothing about it.''

"Then how did I know he was after Leonard?''

The round face worked against the answer and finally gave up in anger. "That son of a bitch!"

Whistling unevenly through his teeth, Billy crossed from the bedroom carefully carrying a page from his notebook. "I think the lab might be interested in this powder.''

"What powder?" Martinez sprang forward, and Wager, using the heel of his hand to leave no bruise, punched his forehead and again knocked him back to the couch.

Billington held the paper just out of reach so Martinez could see its surface. "This stuff that looks like heroin.''

111

"Hey, man, I don't have none of that around here."

"Detective Billington just found the evidence," Wager said.

"But it ain't mine—somebody put it there! *You* put it there!"

"It's our word against yours."

"But you put it there!"

"We'll lie in court, Frankie. Who do you think they'll believe?"

"We won't even have to go to court to fix you up, Frankie-baby. All we do is put your bust in the newspapers. What's Alvarez going to think: first Leonard gets a tip and skips, then you're popped for possession—of his property. And then you're let off with a big smile and no charges."

Billington tapped the powder into a waxed envelope, sealed it, and signed his initials. "I do believe Mr. Alvarez will think Mr. Martinez was trying to be a partner in the firm."

"That ain't so! You know it ain't so!"

"But will Alvarez?"

"Hey, you guys are framing me—you guys are gonna get me killed!"

"I'll try to control my grief."

"Detective Billington is a dirty cop," said Wager, smiling. "Sometimes I'm ashamed to work with him."

"Aw, you say the nicest things, Detective Wager!" Billy tucked the envelope in his coat and leaned over the frightened man. "We've got you by the balls, Martinez, and the only way you're going to live another couple of weeks is to work for us. You do good for us, we'll do good for you."

"Hey, I can't—"

"You can, *amigocito*. And you'd better. All you have to do is give us information on Alvarez's operation. We'll cover you so nobody knows where the word's coming from."

"Now, hey, now. I ain't no snitch."

"It happens all the time. Look, we know what Alvarez is doing. All we want from you is how. We're going to get him—and everybody with him. And if somebody blows the chance to help us . . ." Wager shrugged.

"Frankie, in his own quiet way, old Gabe is meaner than I am. When the time comes, he'll hang you higher than

112

Alvarez because you turned us down.''

"Look, Francisco." Wager offered him a cigarette from the stale pack he never himself used. "You've got nowhere else to go. You can't ask Alvarez for help—he'd never forgive you for tipping Leonard. And if I have to, I'll see that he finds out about it. If you give us a little information, we'll keep you covered. When the bust comes, we can work a deal. Nobody will ever know—we couldn't operate if we let the word get out on our informants. But if you don't come to us, I'll make sure Alvarez sells a wolf ticket on you.''

"I've seen dead snitches before.''

"It does happen, Frankie. But for you it's going to happen a lot quicker if you don't come over.''

"Yeah—and if I do, then I'm your property. I do what you want once, and then you really got me.''

"We've got you now." Billington patted his coat pocket. "But we don't *owe* you anything yet, so it doesn't make a tiddly-damn to us if you live or die. If you help us so that we owe you something, then we'll look after you. We'll cover for you; you'll get no hassles from us if you don't get too far out, and you'll make a lot of bread from a grateful citizenry. Just think, you could be a civil servant!''

"I could be a dead one.''

"If you don't, it'll be more than 'could,' Francisco. We both know what Anthony's like.''

"Gabe, let's hang it up—I've got a lot of things to do. This shitbird don't want us to owe him. We'll let Alvarez off him and save the taxpayers some money.''

Wager sighed and stood erect.

Martinez swallowed and tugged at the little bunch of hairs at the corner of his mouth.

Wager picked up the telephone and started poking the Rare Things number. "Last chance, Frankie-baby. I'm going to make the call, and then me and Detective Billington are going to walk out of here and you're going to be dead.''

"Hey—wait! Wait a minute, now!" Sweat had started in thin lines on his forehead, and Wager could see Martinez's white shirt quiver from his heartbeat. He held his finger over the last number. "You guys gotta cover—you promised you'd cover me!''

113

"If we *owe* you, Martinez, we'll cover for you."

"OK—oh, God—OK. But you guys will owe me. You'll really owe me!" It came out more like a groan than a sentence.

Billington took a deep breath of relief and sat beside the hunched figure. "Let's have it—let's see if it's worth owing for." He took out his notebook and jotted the date.

Martinez, tugging at the mustache, swallowed again and started in a low, dry voice: "I don't know it all; I've made three or four runs with him, but I don't know how it all works." He stopped and looked at Wager. "Can I get a beer? It's in the icebox."

"I'll get it for you." He opened it and poured it and set it on the phone table near Martinez.

"Alvarez, he's into smack real heavy. The last run I made with him, he bought fifteen pounds of smack."

"Run to where?"

"Juárez. There's this guy Fuzzy Valdez—he's the Mexican connection. I don't know where he gets his. South America, maybe—France, maybe." Martinez shrugged and gulped at the beer.

"How often does Alvarez make a run?"

"Depends on business. It's up to once a month or so now. He's down there now."

"Tell us about your run."

"Well, we get the bread—maybe seventy, eighty thousand in cash—and sometimes pistols and rifles. Saturday-night stuff, you know. Alvarez said that if we could get some automatic pieces we could really clean up—Vietnam war stuff. But he ain't been able to get any yet—the wops have that stuff all sewed up; we been looking. They really want that stuff down south—something's building up, maybe. Anyway, we load up at the store and drive all night and get to El Paso maybe two in the afternoon. Sometimes we stop on the way, it all depends. Anyway, we check into a motel and Alvarez makes a call from a pay booth."

"Which motel?"

"Ramada. Sometimes a Holiday Inn. One of them big ones. Rafael likes to go first class."

"Who does he call?"

"Fuzzy."

114

"And then?"

"We have a few drinks and crap out awhile. Then Rafael tells me to sit tight and he goes to the meet. Then he comes back and tells me where to pick up the stuff; I go get it and bring it back. He never touches the stuff."

"You carry it back to Denver?"

"Yeah. Rafael only sees it twice—once at the buy and once at the cut."

"How do you bring it back?"

"Sometimes by bus, sometimes on a plane. I don't know what it's going to be until he gives me the tickets."

"He never delivers to customers himself?"

"I only know of once or twice. He might get a call from a big customer he knows personally who won't take it from anybody else. But that's all. Say, can I have another beer?"

Wager poured another one. "Where does Alvarez take these calls?"

"At the store. He does all his business at the store, but the stuff never goes there."

"Where does he stash it?"

"He's got apartments all over town—Alvarez is smart, man! You'll never get him with the stuff on him. Like, when I make a run, you know, he gives me a key and an address, and I go from the airport or bus station to that address and just leave the stuff in a closet and then take the key down to the store and give it to him."

"What about the cut?"

"Yeah, he's always there for that. Sometimes Anthony or Henry or maybe one or two other people that I don't know, they usually do the cut and make the deliveries. I help with deliveries sometimes. But Rafael's always there to supervise the cut. I been at the cut maybe three or four times."

"Do they set up the cut from the store?"

"Yeah, Rafael calls everybody and tells them which apartment, and they all meet there."

"He never keeps anything at the store?"

"No, man, Rafael's not dumb. He does all the dealing there, but none of that stuff ever leaves the apartment until a deal is set."

"How's the deal handled?"

"Well, Anthony or Henry or somebody might get a call, or

some dude might come into the store and want a buy. Rafael tells them where to leave the money—up front, usually. Or else they bring the money to the store. Then the dude calls the next day and Rafael tells him where to pick up the stuff. If there's more money coming, somebody will meet the dude at the drop and get the rest of the payment."

"But never Rafael?"

"Never."

"Does he have steady customers?"

"Sure! Even some Anglos and blacks. Rafael deals in good stuff; everybody knows it."

"He cuts it thin, doesn't he?"

"Thin? Hell, no—fifty percent. You can't keep customers if you rip them off that way. Alvarez, he's too big time for that little crap."

Then one of the ounce men had cheated Labelle; a little here and a little there, just enough for an extra balloon or two. "Give us some names."

Martinez finished his beer and looked at Wager, who took another from the refrigerator and carried it to the seated figure. "Ernie Sandoval's a big one; he's always ready to buy. I seen Lumpy Gallegos in the store, too, and, ah, Joe Fernandez and this nigger, Spider Robbins."

"Roland Robbins?"

Martin shrugged. "They just called him Spider."

"All these people come to the store?"

"Yeah, but there's a lot more dealing on the phone. Rafael don't like too many people hanging around the store."

"What are the addresses of the apartments?"

"I don't know them all, just the one I use. Rafael's got them all over town, but he only gives me the key to one. Say, don't go busting in there—I mean, that's *my* drop! If you guys bust that one, Rafael will know who told you about it!"

"We just want to keep an eye on it. What's the address?"

"It's out in Lakewood, on Virginia Avenue—7620, Apartment 5."

"Who's making the run with Alvarez this time?"

"I don't know—there's a bunch of us. We never see much of each other. He tells us to stay the hell out of the store unless he calls us."

Martinez fell silent and sipped at the beer; Wager glanced

at Billington, who nodded. "Frankie, we do owe you now. Stay cool, don't do anything different. If we want you, we'll call you and set up a meet. In the meantime, you call us at this number when Rafael's ready for another run."

"Hey, I don't always know when he's going unless I'm on it with him. I mean, I just hear he's gone, and that's it until he comes back, and then sometimes I help with deliveries."

"You call us when you hear something."

"Yeah—sure. You guys really do owe me now, right?"

"Right, Francisco, we really owe you now."

9

Denby, still sitting on the Clarkson Street address, answered Wager's call with a bored "No action here."

"All right. We're about two blocks from you; we'll take over."

"How'd you do?"

"Pretty good. I'll tell you about it in the morning."

Denby's transmission paused. "I can wait here for you."

"That's all right. We don't want you late for that movie." He shouldn't have said that, but it felt too good not to. There was no reply, and by the time he and Billington got to the Clarkson address, Denby was gone.

"You don't get along with him?"

"He's not so bad, I guess."

"Is he a good cop?"

"He could be, if he'd just do his job and stop sweating so much."

"Manic-depressive?"

Billy had finished college, a psychology major, and he let it slip occasionally. But Wager didn't hold it against him; he was a good cop nonetheless. "You might call it that—he's either up tight about nothing or cocky as hell over nothing. He can't seem to tell the nothings from the somethings."

"How long has he been a cop?"

"Five, six years."

"That's too long to be nervous in the service."

Wager nodded as they backed into a parking place—probably the one left by Denby—and settled into the boredom of waiting. They talked a few more minutes about the puzzle of a cop like Denby, then gradually fell silent as the sky darkened into the smoke of a late-autumn evening. Streetlights came on, glowing red at first and then hardening into blue. Lights in the houses came on, too: large yellow squares behind roller shades or thick drapes.

Around eight, Billy sighed, "Damn, I'm hungry. Why don't you get a couple of burgers and some coffee? I'll wait for you here."

Wager came back with the hot cardboard boxes and they slouched low in the seat and ate. The smell, fragrant while the heat stayed in the cardboard, turned to the familiar stale, sour odor as the food cooled. Like almost everything else that got stale, Wager thought; and it was the smell as much as the taste that depressed him: so much life spent watching and waiting, so many hours and days and weeks—maybe years, by now— spent on surveillance. Watching scum eddy around the gutters of the city. And more often than not, it resulted in nothing more than heartburn. And farts. He rolled down the window to let the odor escape.

"The landlady said today was rent day?"

Wager tilted his watch to the streetlight: a little after ten. "If he doesn't come soon, she'll be in bed."

"Maybe that's how he pays the rent."

"You didn't see her."

After a while, Billy said, "I should have brought my thermos of coffee. Say, did Denby tell you about coffee being bad for the heart?"

Wager grunted yes.

The local street traffic had subsided; most of the cars going through were on their way from one distant place to another and used Clarkson as a crosstown artery. The Mach-1 was easy to spot as it slowed to turn in to the driveway.

"That's him," said Wager. "That's Anthony's car!" He leafed back through the notebook and double-checked the license plate: BC 3226.

"One male, no passengers. Going up to the front door. About five eight, slender build; I can't see his face."

The silhouette had the springy walk of a younger man, but it wasn't big enough to be Anthony. Wager fished under his seat for the binoculars and rested them on the window frame. The glare of the opening door flashed into the lenses, and he quickly focused on Lucille Trujillo's jaw. She was smiling and saying something to the dark head on this side of the screen door; the door opened and she looked down, took something, and nodded and smiled again. The lips made a "Thank you" shape and she stepped back and closed the door; then the shadowy head turned away and the light caught the profile for an instant before it became dark again. Wager slipped the glasses behind the door and leaned back from the gleam of passing headlights.

"That Anthony?"

"No. I never saw that one before. But it's Anthony's car."

"Must be one of the runners."

They followed the Mach-1 around the corner and down to Speer Boulevard, where it settled into a steady pace that caught the timed lights. "I bet he's heading back to the Rare Things," said Wager. Sure enough, the Mach-1 turned north on I-25 and picked up speed until it reached the Thirty-eighth Street turnoff.

"Beautiful," said Billy.

Wager nodded and fished in his shirt pocket for a contact card. "Here, fill this out in detail—we've got what Kojak calls a break."

"And no scriptwriter to do it for us."

"Only the big Scriptwriter in the sky."

"Goddam cynical Mex."

Wager was in no hurry now; he followed the Mach-1 automatically, staying a block behind, letting it make a light or two, and then catching up casually. He was busy thinking of what this might mean: nothing yet for the courtroom, but a definite tie between a known drop and the Rare Things; another healthy piece of evidence for a subpoena. Good old Rafael: the eyes mocking and the voice thick with overdone sincerity. He couldn't resist taunting Wager, couldn't deny himself the pleasure of gloating, couldn't forget the old rivalries of childhood. Must be something in the blood, thought Wager—something that made it all worth so much more when there was an audience, a competitor to dance in front of, a loser to taunt. Well, he knew that tune, too; he could dance to those guitars.

"He's turning right."

"He'll pull in behind the store." Wager turned a block

121

short and cruised slowly down the alley to watch the distant tail-lights brake and swing behind a jutting wall. He waited a few moments and then drove past the car parked in the graveled lot.

"Beautiful," said Billy again, and logged in the car's arrival.

Wager nodded and turned back past the bar at the end of the block to park across from the dark front of the Rare Things. "Let's give it a few minutes."

"Right."

Rafael had challenged him, and Wager had accepted it. Accepted publicly, in a way, with his second visit to the store. Rafael wouldn't miss the meaning of that; and while it might make him more cautious, it would also mean it was his move. The move would be to push a little more dope a little faster, to score even while he was being watched and so to demonstrate machismo.

The minutes ticked into an hour. Finally, Billy, who had been yawning wider and wider, said, "Let's hang it up—they're probably in there playing poker and eating tacos."

Wager spent the next morning with Billy filling out the affidavit for a telephone tap on the Rare Things. Denby came in around eleven with a report from Ma Bell's records. "The only thing might be this." He pointed to notations of long-distance calls to the same number in Juárez, Mexico. They occurred at fairly regular intervals—at least once and often twice a month for over a year. Most were less than three minutes.

"That strengthens the affidavit," said Billy.

Denby was trying his best not to feel sulky. "Say, you guys really hit it good with Martinez. Congratulations!" He rubbed at his nose with the handkerchief. "But if he's a new snitch, how can you call him a 'previously reliable informant'?"

Billy winked. "We lie a little. Hell, Denby, if every informant we use has to be 'previously reliable,' how would we ever get a new one admitted in court?"

"Besides," said Wager, "I'm the one swearing to it, and he was very reliable about giving me his name."

"Ha-ha," said Denby.

122

Suzy had the half-dozen legal-sized pages typed by early afternoon and Wager took them to Sergeant Johnston. "How soon can this be acted on?"

Johnston read the pages slowly. "Good—this really looks good, Gabe. Let's go see the Inspector."

Sonnenberg read even more slowly, penciling a note here and there in the margins.

"Who's the informant?"

Wager told him. "I haven't used him before, Inspector. But what he says squares with Alvarez's movements. And I think he's too scared to lie."

"Any corroborating evidence from other sources?"

"Nothing I could bring into court. I had two people on it, but one was blown and had to leave town; I haven't had a report from the other one yet."

Sonnenberg carved a notch in the end of a maduro and lit it slowly; he had a ritual of heating the tip before he drew on it. "The DEA has never tailed Alvarez to El Paso?"

"No, sir."

"And customs has nothing on him?"

"Only on Valdez, but they don't want me to touch him. I'm still waiting for routine information to come in on him."

"Hmm." The Inspector gazed out the window toward the gray stone of the capitol building.

Sergeant Johnston cleared his throat. "It's a family operation, Inspector. It would be harder than hell to get anybody into it from the outside. Gabe did real good to get hold of this one informant."

A ring of thick yellow cigar smoke bounced once on the affidavit and lifted heavily into the air. Wager watched it spread wide and curl inside itself; it had almost dissipated when Sonnenberg said, "Well, you did follow that car from the Clarkson drop to the store. It's thin, but we'll give the Rare Things number a try. The residence"—he shook his head—"no chance. Denby's on this with you, isn't he?"

"Yes, sir."

"How's he working out?"

"Fine, sir."

"All right. I'll see if Judge Weinberg's got time this afternoon."

Wager had a midafternoon lunch; Johnston was waiting

123

when he came back. "Let's go, Gabe. Weinberg's ready now."

The hearing was in chambers; Wager was glad to see Sonnenberg come in. The judge nodded to them and pressed an intercom button for a recorder. She came in and set up her portable machine and mumbled a few introductory phrases into the speaker; the judge himself, thin lips scarcely moving, said to Wager, "Do you, Detective Gabriel Wager, swear that the information in this affidavit pertaining to the Rare Things Import Shop and dated 2 October 1973, and signed by you, is true and complete to the best of your knowledge, so help you God?"

"I do, sir."

Judge Weinberg shoved his glasses up with his thumb. "Have you or any other law enforcement officers purchased or attempted to purchase heroin from the suspect, Rafael Alvarez?"

"No, sir."

"Why not? Isn't that the usual procedure?"

"It would be, sir, if the suspect's operation—alleged operation—was not a family thing. He doesn't handle the heroin except at the buy, at the cut, and maybe sometimes for a few people he already knows. I don't think any officer could get high enough in the operation to buy directly from him. We'd only get as far as third, maybe second, echelon people."

Weinberg frowned at the affidavit, then looked up. "I'd prefer to see *all* the routine methods exhausted before granting a telephone tap."

Sonnenberg spoke: "We understand that, Your Honor; but Detective Wager has been on this case for the last two months, and we've been extremely short-handed."

"I hope you're not implying that telephone taps should replace man power and normal procedures!"

"Of course not. I'm pointing out that, given our resources, we *have* followed all available routine avenues. The close-knit nature of the suspect activity—documented in the affidavit—is the real justification for our request. If one of our officers attempted infiltration in the usual manner, the results could easily be fatal to him. These individuals at the top are too well known to each other to be vulnerable to the usual information-gathering techniques."

"I do understand that, Inspector."

"Yes, Your Honor. But you should know, too, that the information which is needed to further the case against the suspects is not available by any other means. The circumstantial evidence clearly indicates a crime in progress at that address. The times and places of meetings, the runs to Mexico, the actual dealings are all discussed by these highly placed individuals only in strict privacy and only over their private telephone at the Rare Things."

"Detective Wager was emphatic enough about that in the affidavit. But are you saying that corroborating evidence from the other informants in unavailable? I see only one lengthy statement in here from a firsthand informant. The remainder appears to be double hearsay."

It was Wager's turn. "I had another reliable informant on the case, sir, but his life was threatened and to protect him I had to send him out of town."

"The informant was afraid for his life?"

"He sure was, Your Honor. And he never got anywhere near Alvarez himself."

The judge said "Hmm" and reached for the old-fashioned pen on his desk. "It's a borderline case, but I'll do it this one time." He dated and signed the affidavit's subscription line and told the clerk to fill in a court order for his verification. "But if the telephone tap does not result in substantial information by the time this court order expires, I will not renew it."

"We understand, sir." They stood in patient silence while the judge, tilting his head back to read carefully through his bifocals, signed the court order.

In the hall outside chambers, Sonnenberg coldly nipped a cigar with his silver cutter. "We used up a lot of good will on that one, Wager."

"Yes, sir."

"Get on over to Ma Bell and set up the tap"—he prodded the unlit cigar at Wager's chest—"and make damn certain that it pays off."

"Yes, sir."

It took the rest of the afternoon before Wager completed the arrangements at the telephone company. Each office he was passed to had to read the order and verify it with someone else, until the final office, high up in the ugly yellow building, finally called Sonnenberg. Wager could hear the squawk of the Inspector's voice from where he sat.

"I can't help that, Mr. Sonnenberg." The man behind the desk wore a dark suit and a medium-wide tie with muted stripes, the kind of clothes that emphasized his anonymity. He passed his hand over the thinning hair on his head. "We have our federal regulations to follow on a matter of this sort, and we also have to follow company procedures in checking this—er—special equipment out of our warehouse. . . . No, not until tomorrow. . . . You said you wanted a pen register, and I'll have it tomorrow. No sooner. . . . Fine—good-bye." He looked at Wager with hostility. "I'll need your signature on this form and a copy of the court order. Your men will have to monitor the equipment—I don't have the personnel to do it."

"Thank you, Mr. Clinton. I'll have a detective over here first thing in the morning."

"Not here! Send him to the properties building on Arapahoe Street."

"Who should he see?"

"Tell him to ask for Mr. Osborne."

The OCD office was closed when Wager returned, and he let himself in with the passkey. The door buzzed louder than usual in the silence of the room, and he was grateful for the building's emptiness that offered a few moments' quiet in a day otherwise filled with endless words. He left a note on Suzy's typewriter about Mr. Osborne and told her to notify Sonnenberg as soon as she came in. In the center of the blotter on his desk lay a thin folder with "El Paso" printed in Suzy's hand; inside was an abstract of the El Paso file on Valdez: place and date of birth, current residences in El Paso and in Juárez, physical description, a list of half a dozen entries in the arrest column and half as many in the conviction column. All before 1968. Wager studied the charges; the last arrest was for transporting with intent to sell—if he had been convicted of that charge, it would have been the fourth major sentence, and that was the handle customs had on him. It was a good one. That, and a free pass across the border. Wager copied the data into his notebook and sat in the silence to feel

126

around the outlines of the plan that was forming in his imagination. Occasionally he made a note or two: names, sequences, special logistical support. But most of the time was spent in what his fellow officers would call daydreaming. And he supposed he would have to call it that, too—even though the daydreams all centered on the case at hand—because they were guesses and possibilities and maybes that very seldom came about. But he enjoyed picturing the variety of ways the pieces of the puzzle fit together; enjoyed starting first with one item and then another, and following step by step the links between the new A and the new Z.

After a while he stretched, mildly surprised at the darkness in the room that made the telephone dial too dim to read; turning on the small fluorescent desk light, he called Billy. The duty watch said he had gone for the day. "Do you want his home number?"

"No, thanks. I'll call in the morning." He wouldn't need help on the Kalamath Street address anyway.

He tried Ray's number; the old man didn't answer. On a hunch, he picked Willy's number out of his coded list of CIs. A man's voice said the name of the bar.

"Is Fat Willy around?"

"I'll ask. Who wants him?"

"Gabe."

In a few moments, Willy's voice wheezed over the line: "Man, I just as soon do the calling."

Wager could picture the linen-suited figure tipping his wide hat to hide his mouth from the bar's other customers.

"I need some information."

"You always do, man. What's in it for me?"

"A letter of appreciation from the mayor."

"Come on, man. My time's worth a lot. What you want and what you giving for it?"

"Meet me at the Frontier in an hour."

"Right."

He tried Ray one more time, but there was still no answer; then he drove to the Frontier. Rosy, showing a long day, managed to smile hello. Wager ordered burritos and a salad, then ate a slow meal and watched the crowd drift through, that unsettled mixture of fresh after-supper arrivals and tired and slightly fuzzy customers who had drunk through the

127

dinner hour. Willy came in around seven-thirty.

"Drink, Willy?"

"Vodka and Seven." He patted a handkerchief at his face with that surprising delicacy some big men have.

Wager waited until Rosy brought it. "What do you know about Spider Robbins?"

A slow, wide grin started across Willy's dark face. "I know I don't want to mess with that mother. He is the original Bad Dude."

"I hear he's tied to a big operation."

"No shit? Well, you know, he's always got something going. A little this, a little that." Willy shrugged. "I ain't paid much attention to him."

"How about starting to?"

"Hunh-uh! I don't want nothing to do with him."

"It's a big operation, Willy."

"How big is big for me?"

"I can go as high as five hundred for the right information."

The lids dropped slightly over Willy's brown eyes and he tipped his face to his drink, the hat brim revealing only the folded flesh under his chin. "I'm interested. What kind of information?"

"Where and when does he get his stuff?"

"No way, man. That's the kind of questions that'll get me wasted. No deal."

Wager ordered another Vodka and Seven, and another mug of dark beer for himself; he nursed it through Willy's second and third drink as they talked of Pat and Mike. Then he came back to the point. "How about this? Get me the addresses that Spider goes to for the next week or so. He's due to get a shipment soon and I want to know his route."

"You don't want much, do you?"

"It's not Spider I'm after."

"I do believe you!"

Wager smiled. "Not this time, anyway."

"You want to know who's supplying him?"

"I know who. What I need are the connections—the chain of evidence."

Willy gazed at his empty drink and Wager ordered another

128

for him. "I'll give you two fifty for the information; five hundred if it pays off."

"Shee-it! It's worth a thousand just to tail that mother for a week. I mean, he ain't no dummy."

"Neither are you, Willy." He unfolded the bills. "We'll call it five hundred. Here's half now, half at the end of the week."

"All's you want is the addresses—you don't want no names of nobody?"

Wager nodded. He could bargain for names later if he needed them.

The Negro drained his glass and stood, showing no effects of the drinks. The money disappeared and so did Willy. Wager finished his beer and left a larger tip than usual for Rosy.

He parked in a dark section of the block just down from the Kalamath Street address and noted the time in his book. Henry Alvarez's Le Mans crowded the driveway beside the small house, and Wager, his stomach gassy from the beer, settled down to watch. He wasn't sure why, but the restless feeling of something uncompleted had led him here. Perhaps because it was the one address in the journal that he hadn't yet studied—a small peripheral piece of the puzzle that most likely wouldn't mean anything, but a loose piece nonetheless. At about nine-thirty, Anthony's Mach-1 rumbled past and nosed in behind Henry's car. The young man went in alone without knocking, and Wager waited and watched. At eleven, the lights of the house went off except for a small bathroom window beside the driveway. Then that light went off, too. Wager noted it and, with a mental kick to his own butt, radioed in, "Any DPD file on Lucero, Anthony, probable address 3422 Kalamath, Denver." Rafael had called him his sister's boy—Wager heard him say it, but had let it go past.

The reply came in ten minutes later: "One count of assault and battery, 30 September '69; suspended sentence—no subsequent arrests or convictions."

"Anything on that charge?"

"Filed by Mrs. Maurice Williams, 3:42 P.M., 17 September, East High School. No aggravating circumstances."

"Ten-four." Anthony Lucero, son of Diana Lucero, nephew to two uncles: Henry and Rafael. And Diana kept house for brother Henry and son Anthony. Wager, settling another fact in the journal, started home. He was pulling into the parking place behind his apartment when his call number came over the radio.

"This is two-one-two."

"Someone at Denver General is asking for you."

"Ten-four."

Denver General was a familiar drive, and he knew where to look for a close parking place. At the night desk, a crisp nurse, whose skin looked dried out from too much antiseptic, nodded and told him the ward number.

The ward nurse was waiting for him. "Detective Wager?"

"Yes."

"He's in room 612. Please don't stay more than five minutes; he's already been questioned by one policeman." In the silence of the dim corridor, their two low voices were the only sound.

"Who is it?"

"You don't know?"

"Nobody told me."

"Raymond Sauer. He was found beaten up, apparently a robbery."

Wager nodded and looked for room 612. Ray lay under an oxygen tent, the faint hiss of the gas the only sound. The other bed in the room was empty. In the faint night light, Ray's flesh was almost the color of the sheet. Both eyes were swollen dark blobs, and his head was wrapped in bandages.

"Ray? It's Gabe."

A small moan as the old man's head turned slightly. Wager had to lean against the cold plastic tent to hear: "Can't see you."

"Who did it?"

Slight wag of the head and another moan: "Two kids."

"Where?"

"Waiting for me."

"Did you say anything?"

Head wagged.

"Did they take anything?"

130

"Not off me." A sigh that passed for a smile. "What's to take?"

"Did you get anything on Alvarez?"

He waited while beneath the bandage the old man's forehead wrinkled with effort. "Nothing." He stopped for a breath that turned into a rumbling cough which jerked his head against the pillow. It was two or three minutes before he could speak again: "Hurts."

Wager waited.

"Asked around. Nothing. Robbins' stuff is good, but no info."

"He never talked about his supplier or his meets?"

"No—wanted to keep his turf." The old man struggled against another cough, lost, and groaned loudly as his head was waggled.

The nurse stuck her head in the door. "Two minutes."

Ray gasped, "Smack . . . from Robbins. My room . . . under second drawer . . . yours."

"OK, Ray. I'll get it. You rest up now."

In the corridor, he asked the nurse, "How bad is he?"

She shook her head. "He's an old man. The doctor was surprised he was still alive."

10

The hotel Ray lived in reminded Wager of Leonard's. There was the same tiny lobby with chairs that were badly stuffed and worse used, the same dusty odor imprisoned by sealed windows and clanking steam heat, the same hall carpets that looked as if they could never have been new. Only the name was different. Wager found the night clerk scrubbing with a brush and a bucket of water at the carpet and wall outside Ray's room.

"Jeez, another detective? Organized Crime Division?" The thick glasses made the clerk's pale eyes look even wider.

"I'd like to look at his room."

"Well...I guess if you're a cop.... What's old Ray got to do with organized crime?" He twisted a passkey back and forth until the latch gave. "Never mind—I don't want to know!"

"Were you on duty when it happened?"

"When ain't I on duty! I was watching Johnny Carson and I hear a yelp-like, and then nothing. So I figured it wasn't nothing until here comes a thump and I think maybe somebody fell on the stairs. We got lots of old-timers who room here, and they're always falling down or dropping dead or something. So up I go—I'm pretty good at the first-aid crap by now—and I get to the second floor and I hear a bunch of scuffling and cussing and more thumping; and I look over the top step and here's these two Chicano kids kicking the shit out of old Ray. Only I didn't know it was Ray then—I couldn't tell who it was all doubled up on the floor and holding his arms over his head like this."

"Did you recognize them?"

"Naw, they had these stockings on their heads so you couldn't see too good what they were like."

"How'd you know they were Chicano?"

The clerk peered at Wager and smiled knowingly. "The
133

other detective, the Italian guy, he didn't ask that.''

''I'm asking.''

''Yeah. Well, they looked Chicano. Anyway, I yelled. 'Hey, what's going on,' and the two dudes cut out down the hall and out the fire escape. Jeez, I must of been nuts—what if those guys had come after *me*?'' He waited for Wager to say what a brave thing he had done.

''You did a brave thing.''

''Yeah, that's what the other detective said, too. Well, I wasn't much thinking about it, you know? Just reflexes. I guess I was lucky.''

''What's the name of the detective who was here earlier?''

The clerk dug into his shirt pocket and took out a business card. ''Cappiello—Crimes Against Persons Division.''

Wager looked through the narrow room and closet, finding no sign of forced entry. The only drawers were in a combination bureau-and-desk crammed across from the bed. ''Ray's door was locked when you got to him?''

''Yeah, the key was in the lock, but Ray didn't get a chance to open it. Say, was Ray working for you? Was he an informant?''

''No. I never met him. Any idea why they'd beat him up?''

''Robbery, maybe. Or just kicks. Hell, it happens all the time around here. Sometimes in broad daylight, but never inside the hotel here before. But these old geezers can't afford no place else.''

Wager casually opened the drawers, rummaging with one hand through the clothes, old letters, and stray yellowed photographs, while his other hand slipped beneath the drawer. He felt the clerk's eyes following him. ''Did you chase the assailants to the fire escape?''

''Hell, no! I mean, there's old Ray bleeding all over the carpet and sounding like he's choking to death, you know. So I ran down and called the cops and a meat wagon, and then came up and tried to help the old guy.''

Under the second drawer he felt the small bundle taped to the grainy wood; closing the drawer halfway, he opened the bottom drawer and thrust his hands deep into it, peeling off the stash above and palming it.

''You looking for something special?''

"Just looking for possible motives. Routine. Was the fire-escape window unlocked?"

"It ain't supposed to be, but I guess it was. I can't look after every little thing around here all the time."

"Did anyone in the next rooms see or hear anything?"

"I don't think so. The Italian guy and some cops asked around, though."

Wager closed the bureau and walked casually around the small room once more. "Show me the fire escape." He slipped the balloons into his pocket as he followed the clerk to the end of the hall. The large sash window had a swivel lock and no screen; it was a simple matter to slip it open with a knife blade. The metal ladder of the fire escape dropped into a narrow dark alley. "Thanks."

"Sure thing. Hey, if anybody's in the lobby, tell them I'll be down in a few minutes. I got to get the blood off while it's still wet. If that shit dries, it'll never come off."

Wager used the lobby pay phone to call the Crimes Against Persons Division. Detective Cappiello was waiting for him with a cup of coffee when he arrived.

"Not a lead, Gabe. The other roomers heard some noises but nobody opened their door. They were afraid to. Why are you in on it?"

"He was one of my snitches."

"I thought so when he asked for you. Can you give me anything?"

"He was trying to get information on a heroin setup." Wager showed him the stash from Ray's drawer and asked for an evidence bag. Filling out the lines, he told Cappiello about Robbins. "The old man didn't want to be caught with this crap in his room."

"That explains why they took time to beat him instead of just knocking him down and robbing him. I thought it might be a thrill beating."

"Entry through the fire escape?"

"Yeah. There's knife scratches, but no prints."

"Was anyone else in the hall before Ray got hit?"

Cappiello checked his notebook. "A lady from 263 said she went to the bathroom and came back two or three minutes before the assault took place." He followed Wager's thought: "That means the two hoods knew who they were looking for."

"Here's some names, but I'd appreciate your being careful on this." Wager jotted down the Alvarez family. "One of these people might have sold a wolf ticket on Ray; he probably asked too many questions. I'd appreciate hearing from you if you run across anything."

"You bet."

He was in the office by nine the next morning; Denby and Billy sat drinking coffee and waiting for him. He told them about Ray.

"They'll probably never clear that one up," said Billy.

Wager nodded and poured himself a cup of coffee from the thermos pitcher; he handed the Valdez folder to Billy. "As far as we know, Rafael's still in El Paso. How'd you like to go down and see what you can find out about Fuzzy Valdez?"

"And I might see Rafael, too?"

"He doesn't usually stay more than a couple days. He's probably on his way back now."

"Well"—Billy drained his cup—"I'd better get moving."

"We'll have your ticket waiting—Frontier Airlines."

"Right."

Suzy made the calls to the airline; Wager poured himself another cup of coffee; Denby fidgeted and finally asked, "What do you want me to do?"

Wager spoke as much to himself as to Denby: "He'll come back and wait until his runner brings the stuff. Then he'll have the cut and set out his stashes. Then he'll start dealing. I guess it's time we started a round-the-clock. Why don't you sit on the Rare Things until he shows up, and then stay with him. I'll take care of the night shift."

"Right!" Denby drained his cup and bustled out the door.

Wager spent the rest of the morning following up the phone tap; he was appalled to learn finally from a secretary that the first set of equipment had malfunctioned, and the company had had to send to Kansas City for backup equipment. It was due in two days. Wager's accent grew heavy as he thanked the young lady very much and promised to call back then.

Through the afternoon, he moved restlessly from his desk

136

to the coffee machine and back again. He was in that frame of mind where he distrusted his thoughts because they just seemed to be another means of passing time. Increasingly aware of the irritation Suzy felt at having him roll around underfoot, he felt his own temper grow shorter and shorter as the time stretched longer and longer. He finished all the reports due and even anticipated as many as he could, then sat awhile staring at the rare sight of a clean desk. Suzy brought him one form to initial: a voucher for Billy's airplane ticket. And then he sat again, listening to the electric clock give its little raw squeak each time the hour hand moved forward. He should be doing something; there should be something to do. But there was only waiting. And coffee. And wondering idly if Denby was right about coffee's effect on the heart. Not that it made any real difference: the fates would take care of things like that anyway. Finally, around four, he told Suzy he was going to eat before relieving Denby.

"Good."

"What?"

The sound of his voice made her explain quickly, "You've been drinking too much coffee. It's bad on an empty stomach."

"I'll be on duty until six tomorrow morning, and then I'll check in around three." He walked slowly across the capitol grounds to the small restaurant that catered to state congressmen when the legislature was in session. The weather had made another change from the dry cold of the last few days, and was now warm and filled with a hazy slanting sunlight that brought the fall migration of sea gulls wheeling at the base of the Front Range. It would be good to be in the hills in this weather, to capture the fleeting warmth of a small meadow tilted on the sunny side of a mountain. Maybe he would take his vacation in the spring; the springtime was almost as nice as these Indian summer days. He watched the afternoon shoppers, tourists, and petitioners walk through the leaves shoaling on the wide lawns surrounding the government buildings. Most of the women wore dark pants suits with wide legs flapping against their heels, but their coats were open to the sunlight and flashed with bright scarves. Like the autumn flowers that huddled in the tundra from the high-country wind. That's what made Indian summer so

137

nice: the certain feeling that it could not last, that it was some kind of gift before the winter came for good. It was the same thing that made life in general so painful that he preferred not to think about it—if something hurt you, it was easier to ignore it. It really was easier that way.

He finished dinner a bit before six and called ahead to Denby as he neared the Thirty-eighth Street intersection.

"I'll be there in five. Let's meet at . . . Thirty-ninth and Utica."

"Roger."

Denby's Fury III was already at the corner when he turned off Thirty-eighth. Wager parked behind him and slid into the rider's seat; the car smelled of cardboard-wrapped hamburgers. "Any action?"

"Not a thing. The place looks like it's closed. Anything from Billy yet?"

"Not yet. He's probably just getting set up; we might hear in a couple of days. Where were you parked?"

"Across from the bar. I couldn't see the back, but I could watch the entry to the alley."

"Good. I'll see you in the morning."

"What time?"

Denby should have figured it out: half of twenty-four was twelve. "Six."

"Jesus. Well, six it is."

He watched the Fury wheel around the corner into evening traffic, and then made one pass down the alley before picking a slot at the opposite end of the street from Denby's former position. Anthony's Mach-1 was parked behind the Rare Things; the Texas car belonging to Fuzzy Valdez was gone. That was probably the one Rafael drove down to El Paso this time. Noting it in his book, he sank down against the seat and began the night's watch.

In the gray dimness of morning, he saw Denby's car, almost alone, coming down Thirty-eighth. His radio popped with the detective's voice: "Meet you at the same place." This time, Denby slid into the car. "Anything?"

Wager shook his head. "A couple of people came in at ten-thirty-two and then everybody went home at eleven-five." He tried to cover a yawn.

"See you this evening."

138

"Six."

The alarm roused him at two, and that told him how tired he was—usually he woke up ten minutes before it went off. He shaved and arrived at the office a little after three. Suzy was on some errand, but a note anchored on his desk by the unused ashtray said, "Call Agent Hartnoll, customs. Urgent."

"Gabe here, Howie. I got your message."

"And I got a call from the El Paso authorities. It seems somebody's put a tail on Fuzzy Valdez."

"*Qué más?* What's that have to do with me?"

"Valdez doesn't like it and neither do the El Paso people. If Valdez looks hot, it'll scare away all his contacts."

"El Paso's a little out of my jurisdiction, Howie."

"The tail is Billington, from the Denver DEA office. Our people made damn sure who it was."

"I'll be darned! I wonder what old Billy's doing down there!"

"Goddam it, Wager, he's working with you on something and you know it! I called the DEA people and they said he was TAD to your division."

"That's right. And the only reason he's down there is because we did not get the help we needed from your people."

"Look, Gabe, I'll help you all I can. You know that. But Valdez is a sensitive issue and he's out of my hands. El Paso is strung out because Billington's nosing around down there, and they're really leaning on me about it. Gabe, will you do me a favor and call him off?"

With any luck at all, Billy would be finished by now. "I'll think about it. But you're going to owe me one, and by God I'm going to collect on it."

"I'll pay, I'll pay."

"Billy's due to call in soon. I'll see what he's got."

"Thanks a lot, Gabe. I really mean that."

But Billy had not called by five; Wager told the duty watch where to find him and left to relieve Denby. After a quick supper, he radioed ahead: "Anything?"

"Negative."

"See you tomorrow."

"Roger."

139

Denby passed in his car with a tired wave of the hand as Wager took up his position.

Just before eight, Wager's call number came over the radio. The duty watch gave him an El Paso telephone number to call, and Wager drove the three or four blocks to a pay phone. He used the division's credit number and noted the time and call in his book. Billy's voice came faintly over the wire: "I located him. I've got an idea of where he operates here and across the border. He has a residence on both sides."

"Did Rafael show up?"

"I didn't see him, but Valdez was driving the car with the Texas plates, CVM 389. Wasn't that the one behind the Rare Things?"

"Yeah. That's good. Listen, El Paso customs people found out about you and they've been raising holy hell. Come on back and we'll pull things together tomorrow."

"I thought Valdez spotted me; it's tough to trail somebody in a town you don't know. Crap. I'll get the ten-o'clock flight and be at your office in the morning."

"Make it around noon—I'll be on duty all night."

"Will do."

He stopped under a giant neon cowboy hat and picked up two roast-beef sandwiches and a carton of coffee, then drove back to the Rare Things and ate and watched. At 12:25, things began to happen: Rafael's Firebird turned in to the alley behind the store, followed shortly by brother Henry's Le Mans; Alvarez might have come back on the same flight as Billy, the 10 P.M. Which meant that the heroin was on its way and the family was gathering to start operations. Wager cursed Ma Bell and waited. At 12:30, Billy's voice came over the radio: "I'm back. I thought I saw Rafael at the airport, but I'm not sure. I thought I'd let you know, though."

"He drove up about five minutes ago. You maybe had the same flight."

"I had the tourist section; he probably went first class. You want me to come by?"

"Yeah, let's talk."

After a while, a pair of headlights glided up in the rear-view mirror and switched off. Billy opened the door. "Jesus, this thing smells like a dead horse!"

"Call it a dead cow—I hope. You want to put in some overtime?"

"My soul belongs to Jesus, but my body belongs to the state. What do you have from the phone tap?"

Wager told him what had happened.

"Oh, my God."

"Let's get what information we can. How about watching the alley, and we'll see if he leads us to some addresses?"

"We can't justify a search warrant. If we caught them with the dope shoved up their ass, we couldn't get it into court."

"Who said anything about arresting them? They made it home free this time; let's just see what they do."

Billy set himself behind the bar and Wager watched from the street side. At 1:55, Billy radioed, "Two men are getting into the Le Mans. You want to follow them?"

"You take it. I'll wait for Rafael."

"Roger."

Wager sank down in the seat and tilted the rear-view mirror to watch the Le Mans, followed at a distance by Billington, disappear down Thirty-eighth. Then he swung around the block to place himself in view of the rear door. Once the door half opened and Anthony poured a glass of something on the ground. Then it closed again and Wager waited. At 2:27, the door opened again and three figures came through as the light went out. Rafael left first, turning right to Thirty-eighth; Wager peered through the bar's glare but no Firebird passed. He probably turned east on Thirty-eighth. As soon as Anthony's Mach-1 started, Wager swung through the bar's parking lot and jammed down on the gas pedal. Ahead were three sets of taillights, the second belonging to the Firebird, which Wager followed.

It went straight home.

And left Wager to sit flat and disgusted at the entry to the small cul-de-sac surrounded by ranch-type houses all dark but one. He watched while lights spread one by one through the house, and then one by one turned off to leave it dark with sleep. Hail the returning businessman.

Billy was waiting for him when he came into the office the

next day. "I've got three addresses from last night. First was the Royal Lodge Apartments at 4710 Kipling, number 58; they both went in for about ten minutes. The second was 675 Julian, where Henry let off the guy who was with him. The third must have been his home, 3422 Kalamath."

"It is. Did you see Anthony's car there, too?"

"The Mach-1? No. Does he live there?"

Wager nodded. "Did you get a look at the one with Henry?"

"Too dark. That Kipling address might be a good one to start with."

"Let's get legal." He knocked on Johnston's doorframe; the sergeant looked up. "We need a *duces tecum* for an apartment at 4710 Kipling."

The balding head nodded and he pulled open a desk drawer filled with forms. "You getting somewhere on Alvarez?"

"We want to look at some addresses. And how about seeing if you can get the phone tap redated for tomorrow?"

The sergeant paused in filling in the form for subpoena of records. "That might be hard to do."

"The phone company screwed up on the equipment. It won't be in operation until tomorrow, and I hate like hell to lose any of that thirty days."

"I'll ask. But don't count on getting it. What's the ground for suspicion?" He pointed to the form.

"The suspect was followed to that address where he behaved in a suspicious manner. We believe it's being used for harboring drugs."

Johnston finished the pages. "I'll be back in a few minutes with a signature. Have a cup of coffee."

On the way out I-70 to the Kipling address, Wager fit Billy into the twenty-four hour surveillance on the Rare Things. He could relieve Denby at two; Wager would relieve him at ten at night. It was the best they could do until they had more men.

The Royal Lodge Apartments was one of the many new complexes sprouting up at the edge of Denver. The raw brick walls were polka-dotted with used bricks to make them look older, and concrete beams painted brown gave a faintly English touch. The entryway was capped by a gray plastic shield with a helmet and crossed swords; a small copy would

142

look good over Wager's fireplace. He liked that kind of stuff.

Wager found the manager's rooms just across the pool from the clubhouse. "Apartment 58? Records?" He was in his late thirties, tall and sandy-haired, and Wager guessed he had a way with some of the single girls and divorcees who lived there.

"We have a subpoena to produce the records."

"We seldom see anybody in there. Mr., ah"—he glanced at the folder—"Dominico travels a lot."

Wager copied the lease agreement for one Joseph Dominico, who listed his occupation as salesman at 1543 W. Thirty-eighth; reference, Diana Lucero, 3422 Kalamath. "It's the same as Francisco's lease," said Billington. "Except for the car: Henry's license number." He showed the manager a copy of Henry Alvarez's photograph. "Is this Joseph Dominico?"

"Yes—it sure is! Say, I hope this guy's not gonna get busted here. I mean, we're a new place, you know, and we got a image to keep."

"What kind of image?"

"Well, wholesome singles. Secretaries, teachers, salesmen, junior execs, some college students—you know, the happy-swingers bit."

"I'll make a deal with you. Let us have a look at the apartment and we won't hurt your image."

"No way, man! Your warrant's for the records only. I let you in, I could lose my job!"

"We could take time to get a warrant. But if we do, it's a public document, and reporters are really sneaky, dirty guys. There will be no way we can keep your address and the name of the apartments and maybe even your name as manager out of the papers."

"Is that a threat?"

Wager smiled. "It's a fact."

The manager's fingers scratched through his hair and then brushed it quickly back over the balding spot on his crown. "Aw, hell, come on. But for God's sake don't touch anything." He led them to the second block of apartments and up a central staircase. It smelled of new carpet and plaster not yet dry. Fifty-eight was one of two doors opening off the small landing at the top. The passkey worked very smoothly.

143

"Jesus," said Billy, "nobody even moved in."

His voice bounced lightly off the empty walls; Wager, shoes loud despite the carpeting, poked through the other rooms: narrow hall with closet, bedroom one way, bathroom the other. A single roll of toilet paper and a wadded towel in the bathroom; no shower curtain. He joined Billy in the kitchen.

"Looks like they do all their living in here." A card table and four folding chairs were centered under the ceiling light. Billy finished poking through the cabinets and drawers. "Some TV dinners in the icebox; some beer and mix and a couple of bottles of booze in the cabinets. Just a basic, simple life."

Wager peered through the shelves above the dishwasher. "What's this?"

"Looks like a shower curtain."

"They don't have one in the bathroom. Do you furnish these with the apartments?"

"No. Renters do their own decorating."

Billington unfolded it on the card table and rubbed a hand over the stiff creases; a tiny film of powder dusted his fingers. "I'll bet they cut the stuff on this."

"Hey, now, the management's not responsible for what goes on in a leased unit!"

"Who said you were?" Wager finished looking through the drawers; Billington carefully refolded the shower curtain and placed it back on the shelf. They led the manager, still protesting, to the door. "*Amigo*—only you know we were in here. We want to keep it that way. You won't have any trouble if this Dominico doesn't find out about our visit. If he does, we'll know who told him."

"I hear you."

After lunch, Billy went out to the Rare Things; Wager was arguing with the telephone company representative when Denby reported in.

"More trouble?"

He hung up. "Nothing new—just letting them know I'm still around. How's the action with Rafael?"

"He came in late this morning, followed by Henry and Anthony. Two other people came in around one: Robbins and some guy I didn't know."

144

"Good old Spider—a known trafficker. Anything else?"

"Nothing. They were all there when Billy relieved me. What's the chances of being issued a camera?"

"Good idea; I should have thought of that before." He asked Suzy to check out the Pentax and the 1000-millimeter zoom lens. "And get half a dozen rolls of Super Ektachrome—thirty-six exposures."

"Do you think these guys were picking up the dope?"

Wager shook his head. "Rafael wouldn't have it at the store. They were probably dropping front money and being told where to pick up their stuff and when." He gazed out the window and over the trees, which a few weeks ago were alive with sun and greenness; now, with the frost and autumn winds, the leaves had been stripped and only a haze of gray limbs thrust over the low roofs of the old district. He, Rafael, and the others had walked to school on those cold mornings, bundled against the north wind, cutting across the flattened weeds of empty lots, shying stones at cans or cats or each other, and always finding something to laugh at. Somehow it seemed a long time since he had found something to laugh at. "Let's take the camera out to Billy. Then I think it's time we visited Martinez."

11

They had to wait for Martinez; Wager finally spotted the short figure hunched in a tan topcoat and walking quickly through the late afternoon's pale light.

"Here he comes. You go down there, I'll take him from behind." He let Martinez get halfway up the worn steps to the apartment and then slid out of the car. "Hello, Francisco. Long time."

Martinez twitched and looked over his shoulder, starting back down the steps until he saw Denby standing in the middle of the sidewalk. He stopped, and Wager noted the man's shoulders rise and fall in a sigh.

"Invite us in, Francisco."

Wordlessly, he unlocked the inner door and the three went to the apartment. Martinez placed the chain and kept his coat on; Denby studied the man while Wager, after a quick prowl through the rooms, sat on the Danish Modern couch. "Any beer in the box?"

The Cantinflas mustache jerked once or twice and finally a dry "Yes" came out. Wager brought back three and snapped the rings. They watched the thick foam well out of the holes; the bubbles crackled faintly in the silence.

"You were supposed to call us when Rafael started dealing again." Wager kept his voice friendly.

"I didn't know about it until today. I swear I didn't know about it."

"But you found out and still didn't call. That doesn't show much concern for law and order."

"I was gonna call when it was safe! That's what I was gonna do right now."

"Sure it was. That's why you were so glad to see us."

"I was gonna call! And you wasn't supposed to come here
147

no more. You said you'd cover me and we'd meet some-wheres else.''

"We got lonesome when we didn't hear from you. And we got a little bitty bit upset when we heard about the deals being arranged.''

"If you heard about it, what do you need me for?''

"Because we heard about it too late, Frankie-baby. Where's the cut?''

The brown eyes slid away from Wager to Denby. "Who's this guy?''

"Detective Denby. He works with me.'' Wager still couldn't manage to call him his partner. "Where's the cut?''

Martinez swallowed some beer. "It's over with. They did it early this morning. But I really didn't know nothing about it until . . .''

"Until what?''

"Until I got a call to set up a delivery.''

"What time this morning?''

"They called me about ten or eleven. They must have started the cut about four in the morning.''

"You've let me down on two things now, Frankie: the cut and your deliveries. If we can't trust each other, we don't owe each other anything.''

"I didn't have a chance! I just now got back; I was gonna call you now!''

"Where was your delivery?''

"At my drop—the place over on Virginia Avenue. But you said you wouldn't work that one. You said you'd cover me!''

"Since you didn't call us, we'll do what we have to.''

The round face turned a yellow-green color and he tried once or twice to stand, but his knees would not work. "For God's sake, don't sell me out, Wager. I gave you a lot of information last time and you said you owed me. You said you really owed me!''

Wager stood and drained his beer, belching slightly. "Gee whiz, we did say that, didn't we?'' Squeezing the can flat, he bent it over his thumb and set it rocking by the telephone; then he leaned over and stared flatly into Martinez's eyes, no longer hiding his contempt. "All right, Frankie, we won't do anything with your drop this time. But it makes us even, you son of a bitch, and you better produce from now on, because right now I don't owe you a goddamned thing."

Martinez licked at his lips and swallowed. "Yeah. Right. Thanks a lot, Wager."

"You will tell me ahead of time when Rafael's making another run."

"I'll try. I sure will try!"

Wager smiled. "If Alvarez leaves town without me hearing about it first, you'd better leave, too, *comprendes tú?*"

For the first time, anger hardened through the fear in Francisco's eyes; and it made Wager almost laugh at the petty little things that mattered to scum who had sold away honesty and courage and loyalty: Francisco felt insulted by the familiar form of the verb. "Thanks for the beer."

In the car, Denby cleared his throat. "You sure leaned on him!"

" 'Let them hate as long as they fear.' "

"Who said that?"

"Hitler or Nero or somebody. Maybe Mayor Daley."

"You think he'll tip us on Rafael?"

"If he doesn't, he's a dead man. I wasn't pulling him through the grease on that. And he knows it."

"Man, someday one of those dudes is going to try and waste you."

"It beats watching TV. Go over your notes for this morning again."

Denby flipped through his small notebook and reread the entries on arrivals. "They all came in around eleven-thirty; Rafael was first, and then Henry and Anthony. Then Robbins and his accomplice at one-five. They were still there when I was relieved. What about last night? What did you see?"

"Not e-goddamned-nough. They closed up just after two and Rafael went home; and I must have really blown it. They probably set up the cut and then went home and pretended to go to bed. Then they sneaked out to wherever and did it early this morning."

"They know we're on to them?"

"They have to suppose so. And maybe they've seen us hanging around the Rare Things." Or Fuzzy Valdez tipped

149

them about Billy. Or maybe even Francisco—no, not him. He'd have too much explaining to do. Maybe it was routine security and that's what they do every time. Maybe. Too many maybes. What was certain was that Wager didn't have enough man power to do the job without screwing it up; it was time for some real support or the whole thing would be lost.

"Where are we headed?"

"I think it's time to pull back until we can do things right."

"You mean just let the deal go through?"

"There'll be another time."

Denby was silent as they drove up to Billy's empty car parked beside it for a minute or two, they pulled around the corner and waited. A few moments later, Billy walked up to them. "You called?"

"What's going on?"

"Not much. Spider and the other black came out around three and headed east on Thirty-eighth. I got some pictures of them. Nothing since then."

"They held the cut this morning. I screwed up and they got away from me after I thought they went to bed."

"Are they on to our surveillance? Jesus, I could swear nobody spotted me."

Wager shrugged. "I don't know. But let's back off until we get the right kind of support. We don't want to spook the bastards."

Billy looked down between the car and curb and spit thoughtfully. "You don't think we've got enough now?"

"Add it up the way a jury of civilians would see it."

He nodded. "I guess you're right. Goddamn, we're so close!"

"We still have the phone tap and some addresses." And Rafael's machismo; it wouldn't be long. "Let's do this: Denby, you go sit on the Clarkson address where Labelle picked up her stuff; Billy, move over to the Kipling Street apartment—maybe it'll help you improve your image. I'll take a look at Francisco's drop on Virginia Avenue. No busts—let's just see if we can tie the Alvarez family to some convicted dealers."

"You told Martinez you wouldn't use his place," said Denby.

"We don't owe that bastard anything."

Billington grinned at Denby. "That's his colorful Chicano heritage coming out: the Inquisition, Aztec sacrifices, conquistadors, a few peon slaughters."

"Don't forget the grape boycott."

"The crowning glory! How long do you want us on these places?"

"Let's give it until midnight, maybe one o'clock. If they have the buyers lined up, they might be moving the stuff fast. Maybe we'll have some luck. If not, we'll get a night's sleep for once."

"Right. See you tomorrow."

Wager drove Denby to the unit's parking lot. Instead of going to his car, Denby fit his key into the glass door of the nearby building. "I better call the wife," he said to Wager; "she was expecting me."

Wager nodded. "See you tomorrow."

The apartment on Virginia Street was one of ten, five up and five down, in a pink stucco building that looked more like a cheap motel than an apartment house. Number 5 was the last on the bottom row. Anyone inside could see the entry to the parking area out back. Wager turned around in the street and drove up a small hill to a gas station; the attendant filled the car while he studied the darkening neighborhood. The glare of Federal Boulevard blotted the eastern sky, but here, away from the main artery, the evening had that quiet feel of a neighborhood settling down to supper. One by one, rows of streetlights silently flicked on, the older ones dull yellow bulbs, the newer ones orange gleams that seemed to make the shadows thicker. Lights glowed in the windows of several of the pink apartments, but number 5 remained dark. After cruising two or three times around the block, he finally settled on a space at the end of a weedy half-block and sank down on the seat to watch and listen to the radio traffic of District 4. At ten o'clock, the gas station closed; Wager gave it another half-hour and then pulled into the shadow of the gas-station office. From the low ridge, he could better see Apartment 5 and the driveway. At 11:10, a metallic brown Duster with wide slicks nosed into the driveway beside the apartment, then turned to park by the back door. Wager focused the glasses on the license plate, catching Colorado AR 3 before the light went out. A moment later, the apartment lights flashed on and a dark figure pulled down the roller shade at

151

the window. Wager noted the time and the man: Roland
Robbins. A second shadow, shorter, moved across the shade
covering the kitchen window; then the dull glow remained
unbroken. The meet took ten minutes; when the lights turned
off, Wager started his car and waited, swinging in behind the
Duster as it paused at a stop sign before turning toward
Federal. He called in the license number, and by the time he
was in the boulevard traffic the answer came back: "Robbins, Roland Griffin, 2615 Clermont, Denver. No warrants.
He does have a DPD number."

He followed the Duster north through the pulsing neon of
the boulevard, then east on Colfax to Capitol Hill. It paused
near Tremont to let the rider out, and Wager nodded to
himself when he saw the familiar tan topcoat; Martinez
walked quickly toward the Silver Lode Bar and Robbins
continued east on Colfax to turn north on Clermont. Wager
stayed with him until he saw the Duster pull into the narrow
driveway beside 2615. He slowly passed the single-story
brick house, watching from the corner of his eye as the tall,
gangly Negro, still sitting in the car, waited. Wager turned
right around the block and came back down Twenty-sixth to
park at the curb with the house just in sight. The Duster was
empty now, the porch light glowing whitely over the small
landing at the front of the house. Robbins would spend the
night cutting the dope again and measuring it into balloons for
street sales. And tomorrow they would be all over East High
and Manual. And even the nearby junior high schools:
Smiley, Grove, Cole. On the map in his head, Wager could
see the schools marked in orange and forming a neat circle
around Robbins' house; and he remembered the sneering grin
on Robbins' face when the pusher walked, free, out of the
station. He could be nailed right this minute: neither the toilet
of his house nor the toilet of his throat would be big enough to
get rid of all the dope this time. He could be nailed right now.
But he wouldn't be. Wager sighed and started the car and
pulled into the slow traffic of the street: Alvarez was the
bigger target.

He came into the office early enough to surprise Suzy.
"Has Denby or Billington come in yet?"
"No. Do you want me to call them?"

He shook his head. "If they're not in by ten, give them a call." He dialed Masters; a voice he didn't recognize told him that the detective wasn't in yet and asked if there was a message.

"Just tell him Spider Robbins got a shipment."

"Will do."

He dialed another number. It was answered in half a ring: "Otero."

"This is Gabe, Phil. Do you have anything yet?"

"We're just getting the tape now. You want to come over and hear it?"

"I'm on my way." He left word for Billington and Denby that he would be back at ten-thirty; they were to wait for him.

In the small, windowless room that served as a laboratory, Phil Otero sat behind his collection of tape decks, speakers, and amplifiers. "There's the one we picked up this morning. Just let me finish logging it in." He completed the evidence tag and copied the serial numbers into the record. "OK, let's run it."

They listened to the clicking of the pen register, Otero slowing it down to be certain of the number: 632-6081. After the rattle of the bell, a voice, flattened through the telephone wires and the recorder, answered hello.

"I just got in from El Paso. You ready?"

"Any time. What you got?"

"The usual."

"You want the money at the same place as last time?"

"No—another place. Put it in some envelopes and leave it in the mailbox at 4710 Kipling, Apartment 58. By midnight."

Otero mumbled, "We got a federal case."

"OK—4710 Kipling, Apartment 58. Where do I pick it up?"

"I'll call you when we've got the money."

The tape clicked silent as Alvarez hung up, then clicked on again with the next series of numbers: "I just got in from El Paso. You ready?" The voice was slightly different from the first—possibly Henry's.

"Why not, man? I got a lot of hungries."

"That's Spider Robbins," said Wager.

"How much?"

153

"The same."

"Put the money in some envelopes and leave it in the mailbox at 675 Julian Street."

"No way, man. I bring it by the store like always. Half in front and half when I get the stuff."

The line paused in silence, then hissed open with the sound that comes when a hand is lifted from the mouthpiece. "OK, noon tomorrow."

"I'll be there."

There were four more calls, all with the same pattern. Wager had Phil replay the tape in slow speed to double-check the phone numbers.

"There's no mention of heroin anywhere. It won't be worth much in court, Gabe."

And so far they had no evidence of heroin dealing at any of the addresses mentioned on the tapes. "Can you make a copy for me?"

"No problem. You want it now?"

"I'd like to take it with me."

At the office, Suzy had two messages for him, the first from Denver General about Ray. He called the extension she gave him. "This is Detective Wager. I have a message to call you about a patient, Ray Sauer."

"Oh, yes." The nurse's voice reported facts with just enough respect for the injured and dying. "Mr. Sauer slipped into a coma this morning at five-thirty, and passed away at eight-twelve. His injuries were terminal."

"Has Detective Cappiello been notified?"

"Yes, he has. He asked me to call you."

"How about the next of kin?"

"There was none listed. Do you know of any relatives?"

"No." It was Cappiello's worry now; another unsolved murder.

The second message was from Fat Willy—call him. Wager put it aside; Willy could wait for the other half of the fee.

Billington came in. "What's the word?"

"Old Ray just died."

Billy wagged his head. "He was one of your better snitches."

"He was. What did you find out last night?"

"One piece of action. About midnight, some dude put something in the mailbox. I figured it was a payment."

"No one came to get it?"

"I left at one, like you said. If they came, it was after that."

Denby walked in and said good morning and poured himself half a cup of coffee, then scrubbed at his nose with the handkerchief. "I think it's the coffee I'm allergic to. But I can't do without it."

"Did you come up with anything last night?"

"Yeah. About eleven-thirty, Anthony's Mach-1 drove up. But Anthony wasn't driving. It was some other kid I didn't recognize. About five eight, slender build, dark complexion. Probably Chicano, but I couldn't see him too well."

"Must be the one we saw paying the rent," said Billington.

"What happened?"

"He went in and turned on the lights. At around midnight, I saw this light blue VW van go around the block about three times." He read from his notebook, "Colorado RT 4019, registered to: last name, Olssen; first name, Carter; 6214 Newcomb Drive, Arvada, Colorado. No warrants, no DPD number. The driver was alone, a male Caucasian about six foot; slender build, long hair light in color, around twenty-five years old. This guy finally parked down the street and walked back and forth a couple of times and then went up and knocked. He went in at twelve-eighteen and came out at twelve-thirty-two, got into the VW and left. The other guy came out at twelve-fifty and also left. That was it; I came home about one-thirty."

Wager gazed out his window as Denby finished his report; the distant branches of the trees were almost invisible against the gray sky. Only their gray blur showed over the low roofs. He sighed and tapped the flat box of the recorder tape. "Suzy, get me something to play this tape on, and find out when the Inspector can see us."

Denby asked, "Do you want me to tip the Arvada police on the Olssen guy?"

"Not yet. We don't want to scare Alvarez by busting all his buyers."

"It seems a shame to let the bastard get away with it."

"Sure it does. But maybe we can work things next time to get the whole bunch."

Billy grinned. "The old Chicano is a dirty plotter."

"If we can get the support." He looked at Denby. "And if we have the patience."

Sonnenberg's office smelled thick with old cigar smoke, and he was carving a notch in another maduro as the detectives entered. His eyebrows bobbed an invitation for Wager to speak.

"Here's the first tape, sir. I'd like to hear it." He plugged in the machine and threaded it.

Sonnenberg creaked back in his chair and watched his cigar smoke rise as the voices ran mechanically from the speaker. When it ended, he said, "Is that all?"

"So far."

"No names, no use of the word 'heroin,' no way to connect Alvarez and the dope?"

"Henry rented one of the apartments that was mentioned."

"It's still circumstantial. I hope you do better on the other tapes."

"I don't think we will."

"Why not?"

"I think this is most of the action for this run. I'm hoping he'll say something about another run."

"He better say it in the next twenty-four days."

"You don't think we can get another month?"

"With this?" A thick ring of cigar smoke. "Judge Weinberg refused to redate the affidavit. He doesn't like phone taps."

"What about a voice print?" asked Denby. "I read that some guy up at the university has a machine that can identify voices."

"It makes no difference whose voice it is; nothing's said about heroin."

Wager gave him the facts of Denby's and Billington's surveillance.

"But none of you actually saw heroin exchanged?"

"No, sir."

"No case."

"With a little support, we can get him on the next run. We know how he operates now."

"Um. How much is a little?"

He had it figured out. "Thirty, thirty-five men."

"Jesus H. Christ! Why don't you ask for a tank division!"

"Do you have one?"

"Don't get wise-assed with me, Wager. You're asking me to pull a lot of people off the streets and off other cases."

"It will be worth it if we get him."

The Inspector drew on the cigar and looked out his window to the capitol building across the street. In the overcast, its gray stone seemed heavier and darker than usual. "What do you have in mind?"

"I'd like a round-the-clock tail on Alvarez starting now. That'll take four men. When we get the word he's going to El Paso, I want to follow him; me and Billington . . . and Denby. Then we'll need someone covering the airport and bus terminal to pick up on the courier when he comes back. Then we'll need all the men we can get: on the courier, on Alvarez, on the Rare Things, on the phone tap. And some backup people, too, for a network. It's the only chance we'll have to get him at the cut."

"You'll want most of them for a week or so."

"Yes, sir. Maybe less."

"When you get something worthwhile, I'll see what I can do. Can I have this tape for a while?"

"Yes, sir."

Back in their office, Denby slapped Wager's shoulder. "Man, we've got him!"

"Not yet, we don't. Billy, how about twisting Martinez's tail so he doesn't forget us."

"I'm on my way."

They were all on their way. Or at least it felt like it for a day or two. Until the surveillance settled into its pattern and the tapes lived up to Wager's prediction, with only an occasional deal implied here and there. Wager, taking his turn with Alvarez, spent the late nights and early mornings at the Rare Things or down the street from Alvarez's home. Routine: Alvarez at the store until 9 or 10 P.M., then home; sometimes he left earlier and went to a movie or a restaurant with his family. A good home-loving parent, taxpaying citizen, probably played church bingo, too. At 7:45 in the morning, Alvarez's three kids left for school; and he left the house about 9 A.M. Usually to the store, sometimes shopping with the wife. A week. Two weeks. Patience and more patience. On the calendar at his desk, Wager crossed out the days leading up to the circled ''30'' that marked the end of the wiretap. On the eighteenth, he went to see Sonnenberg.

''We need that extension.''

''Alvarez still sitting on his tail?''

''He probably knows we're watching him, but he's going to have to move soon. He's got customers depending on him.''

''What do you have from the tapes so far?''

''A few more deals, but not much that will hold up in court. Billy's come up with something, though: one of his DEA agents made a heroin buy in the Pecos Lounge; he was told that if he wanted more he could call 632-6081 and order it. That's the number of the Rare Things.''

''That'll help with Weinberg. Can you get it in an affidavit? Firsthand?''

''I can try. I've got some addresses from the phone numbers on the tapes.'' He showed Sonnenberg the list. ''The ones with the stars are known traffickers.''

''OK, that's something more. But you'd better know there won't be another one, no matter what evidence comes up.''

''I hope to hell we won't need another one.''

12

Otero started it with a midafternoon call: "My man contacted me about five minutes ago, Gabe. The Rare Things placed a call to Juárez, Mexico, to the residence of Ricardo Valdez. He got a price of sixty thousand for four kilos. The Juárez number said he'd call back when the stuff was ready."

"Thanks, Phil. Let me know as soon as Valdez sets up a date." It could be a few hours or a few days; he took the information to Sergeant Johnston, who started making his phone calls.

"Suzy, get the motor pool—I want a pickup truck with a camper on it. With plates from El Paso County." A little humor never hurt. "See if they can have it ready by tonight. I'm not sure how long we'll need it."

Billy was off duty—he had a morning shift—and Denby was with Alvarez and due to check in at four. He left word with the duty watch for both men to call him, and then he telephoned Martinez.

"Things are starting to happen, Frankie-baby. I don't want you to miss anything we should know."

"I won't."

"You'd better not."

Once again he went over the procedures list, once again trying to outguess all the possibilities, once again with that inevitable feeling of something forgotten. His phone rang; it was Denby. "Something up?"

"Alvarez is setting up a buy in Juárez. What's he doing now?"

"He's been at the store all afternoon. Same routine, no customers."

"No extra traffic?"

"Not a thing."

"Stay around home when you get off duty. He might start the run any time."

"OK. Say, ah, any idea how long it might be? I ought to tell the wife."

"Depends on how fast he drives and how quick he deals. Four or five days, maybe."

"OK."

Just before quitting time, Suzy told him the motor pool called. "The truck's ready. You'll have to sign it out."

It took forty-five minutes to fill out the paperwork and transfer the paraphernalia from his car to the camper: camera and lenses, binoculars, an extra box of rounds, the handcuffs that were always getting lost somewhere under the car seat. Back at the now quiet headquarters, the duty watch told him Billington had telephoned. "He said for you to call him at home."

One of Billy's young sons—either Chris or Erik—answered, and Wager could hear the high-pitched "Daddy, it's for you."

"This is Gabe. Alvarez is setting up the meet in Juárez."

"When do we leave?"

"It could be soon, it could be in a few days."

"I'll be ready."

But it wasn't soon. The afternoon, the evening, the next morning, and the time after that stretched into the worst kind of waiting; everyone seemed to be leaning over a cliff, tensely holding back until the word came to jump. Even Suzy began to answer the telephone with a curt voice, and Wager had to start sucking mints to cut the acid coffee that he kept pouring into his stomach. Otero grew tired of answering the telephone—"Gabe, I'll call *you* as soon as I hear anything. I said I would and believe me, I'll *do* it." And Wager grew just as tired of answering Sergeant Johnston's question: "Ed, I don't know when. Tell them they'll just have to stay loose. We're just as eager as they are to get this crap moving." And Denby, between sneezes and coffee, kept wishing he could tell his wife something definite: "She just doesn't like this kind of insecurity."

When Otero's office finally called, Wager was at his apartment sipping a beer and watching Lieutenant Colombo make the guilty confess by popping back into the room and waving a cigar at them.

160

"The call just came through, Detective Wager. Just a minute, I'll replay it for you."

A voice with heavy Spanish rhythm came over the crackling connection, "*Qué pasa, hombre?*"

"*Lo mismo.* You ready with it?" It wasn't quite Rafael's voice, and not young enough for Anthony. Possibly Henry.

"Thursday."

"OK—Rafael, he'll call you when he gets there."

The tape clicked silent. Otero's man asked, "You want it again?"

"No. Thanks for letting me know."

El Paso was about six fifty, maybe seven hundred miles: a day and a night or two short day's drive. Wager traced the probable route down from Denver and along the Front Range to Trinidad, then across the state line into New Mexico and up over Raton Pass. Down through Santa Fe and Albuquerque, to run along the Rio Grande and finally angle east to the spur of Texas where El Paso and Ciudad Juárez sat across from each other on the yellow national boundary line. The map also showed a number of smaller roads, narrow blue or dotted bands cutting arcs and elbows off the red trail of the main highway; and a lot of open, empty country where the camper would stick out like a sore thumb. Yet to make the case stand up in court, they would have to be with the suspect every inch of the way, would have to get close enough to identify positively the Mexican connection and the sale; photograph or mark it, if possible; trace the dope back to Denver; and, finally, try to nail good old Rafael with the dope in his pocket. And Denby, who should have known better, was saying Rafael was already in their hands. He poured himself another beer and sipped it through another segment of the TV drama, the part where the bad guy thinks he's on top of it all just before Colombo drops the bomb. But if he'd been asked to say what the TV detective's bomb was, he simply wouldn't have known—his mind was on that red line of a highway wiggling south.

After a while, he called the duty watch at headquarters. "I'll be gone for about an hour. If anybody wants me, get a number. I'll call them back at"—he glanced at his watch—"ten-thirty."

The hour was spent shopping at an all-night food store, Wager loading up the wire cart with cans and boxes of quick

161

foods. At one entrance to the store was the inevitable ice machine and, after storing the food in the camper's tiny cupboards, he slid a couple of blocks of ice into the cooler unit. Eggs, butter, a case of Coors, milk, fresh fruit—all in under the ice compartment. He hoped that one of them would be a good cook. He measured the LP gas and the water reservoirs: both full. The bunks were only bare mattresses—he should get some blankets and towels from the apartment. And toilet paper—he almost forgot the toilet paper. Back into the empty store and aware of the lone clerk's nervous eyes following him up one aisle and down the other. Finally, it seemed done; the truck, spongy on its shocks, rocked heavily up and over the cross streets as he drove back to his apartment, stopping once to top off the gas tank at an all-night Serv-Ur-Self. Then he called in: "Any messages?"

"One. Here's the number."

It was Francisco's. Wager dialed it; it rang twice. "Hello?"

"This is Wager."

"It's about goddam time—I thought you were hot for this!"

"Let's have it."

"There's a buy set for this weekend. Rafael and a friend of Anthony's are driving down to Juárez for the deal."

"When are they leaving?"

"Wednesday morning. The stuff should be back Saturday or Sunday."

"Who's this friend of Anthony's?"

"I don't know his name. I've seen him around is all. Say, you don't sound too excited about this; you know I'm really out on a limb talking to you like this."

"I'm excited. What car are they driving?"

"I can't say for sure. They usually take one from the store and then trade off somewhere for another one."

That was a wrinkle to iron out. "When's the cut?"

"I don't know. It'll be sometime after the stuff cools for a while. Maybe next week, maybe a couple of weeks. It's up to how Rafael feels about it."

"I should be back when Rafael is and I'll give you a call. But if you hear anything about the cut and I'm not around, you call this number and ask for Detective Sergeant Johnston.'' He gave him the duty watch's number. ''Tell him where the cut is and that I said you were to call him. Repeat the number to me.''

''I got it. I ain't a kid.''

''Let's hear it.''

''It's 255-1522.''

''Detective Sergeant Johnston, the minute you hear a thing.''

''Yeah. Hey, now you owe me again, right?''

''If we get that cut, we'll not only owe you, we'll pay you.''

''How much?''

''Ten percent of the value.''

A cautious pause. ''That could be a lot.''

''How much do you think it might be?''

''I heard Anthony mention sixty, maybe seventy big ones.''

That fit. ''Ten percent. And protection if you want it.''

''Jesus, I hope I don't need it. You people couldn't do it anyway—you don't know Anthony. Just pay me and keep your goddam mouth shut.''

''What we owe, we pay.''

''I hope so.''

On Monday afternoon, Sergeant Johnston held a conference: Wager, Denby, and Billington, along with ten members of the task force, crowded into the small room. Johnston introduced the two or three faces that were new and then propped up the organization chart he and Wager had put together that morning. At the top was Rafael's mug shot, with a line running down from him to the smaller pictures of Henry and Anthony. Beside their faces was the label ''Lieutenants.'' Valdez's photograph was on the same row, with ''Supplier'' under his name. The third row held other pictures labeled ''Bagmen'': Francisco, Spider Robbins, Pat and Mike (with a green dot after their names indicating conviction), some blank squares of Unidentifieds. Beneath that were the known bagmen and female associates. Most of the women were young, some even pretty despite the police photograph and the hatred or fear that closed their faces against the camera. All but one were Chicanos; she was a

163

blond Anglo. Wager knew most of them; they gathered like flies on shit, and if you stuck your nose in enough shit, you began to recognize the flies. Along the border of the organization chart, and listed by police district, were the bars and restaurants known to be frequented by the suspects. Sergeant Johnston went through the chart in a stiff voice, adding a comment here and there. Suzy was kept busy filling and refilling the coffeepot.

"Gabe, you want to take the next part? Detective Wager will now go over the next part."

He picked his way forward through the knees and feet. "We have information that Alvarez and an accomplice will make their run Wednesday morning. They may switch cars before leaving the city. What I'd like is for the local surveillance on the store and on Alvarez's home to tail them to the switch, and then—if they do it—to have a new unit pick them up from there. If there's no switch, the original tail should stay with them. The suspects should be followed south as far as Colorado Springs, where Detectives Billington, Denby, and I will be waiting. We guess they'll take the freeway south, but they might take this route"—his grease pencil slid down the acetate-covered map of the state's roads—"State Highway 83, just to see if anybody's following them. We'll be stationed at this point here"—he drew a circle—"just north of the Springs where 83 and I-25 join. There's a little roadside park where people pull over to look at the Air Force Academy, and it's within radio distance of both highways. We'll also try to establish phone contact with unit headquarters. The tail should use the police band to tell us you're coming and on what highway; Sergeant Johnston can let us know ahead of time what kind of car you'll be driving."

"I'll give them yours."

He waited for the ripple of laughter to die. "They probably know that one. Anyway, we'll pull in behind the tail and come up on closed channel two; give us a description of the suspect vehicle and then pull off somewhere in the Springs. We'll take it from there."

There were some questions and suggestions but none of them worth a damn. They seldom were. One of the men, whose face Wager hadn't recognized, raised his hand. "What's the chance of popping Alvarez when he crosses the border with the stuff? Maybe we could get him on a federal charge.''

"We're not sure Alvarez crosses it himself. If he does, we just might tip off customs right then.''

"What about the buy? He's gonna look at the stuff to make sure it's good before he pays off; we might nail him then.''

Billy answered that one: "It'll be in Mexico, and we don't trust the Mexican officials all that much. We know that some of them are owned by local dealers, but we don't know which ones. We just don't want to take a chance on a leak.''

"The only real chance we'll have for a possession charge is at the cut here. When Alvarez comes back from the run, we'll just have to put a lot of people all over the place. Sergeant Johnston will be organizing that end of it while we follow Alvarez, and that's when most of you will be involved.''

There were few other comments; the meeting broke up. Back in their office Billy yawned and scrubbed at his bloodshot eyes. "I'm going home—I've got to get some sleep.''

Denby sneezed and asked, "What about the truck—is it all set for the trip?''

"I picked up some stuff last night. I hope you like Chinese food.''

"I'm allergic to almonds.''

They neared the rendezvous point at seven, just after the late-autumn sunrise. The dawn's brief glare washed against the rock faces of the Front Range, tinting the granite ribs of Pikes Peak to the southwest and turning the scattered mine tailings into scarlet spills here and there across the slope of the range. It gave Wager the hungry feeling he sometimes had when he let himself think of the quiet emptiness of the high valleys; it was a feeling he did not like, but it reminded him too sharply of the other things he would rather be doing. The answer was not to let himself think of that feeling, but to watch the heavy work-bound traffic swinging in long lines down and over I-25 into Colorado Springs and toward the south gate of the Air Force Academy. Wager steered the pickup truck into a gas station and while the tank was filled and Billy and Denby trooped to the rest room, he called Denver.

"Ed? This is Gabe." It was a bad connection and he had to shout through the traffic sounds echoing in the open phone hood. "We're on location. Have you heard anything?"

A faint "Not yet" through the humming wire.

"Here's this number." He read it twice before Johnston had it. "It's a pay phone in a Conoco station at the south gate of the Academy. We'll wait here and you call us when you get word that Rafael's on his way." Damned if he wanted to spend a day waiting for nothing if the tip had been wrong.

When the truck was topped off, Wager pulled up near the telephone and sat in the warm cab listening, while Billy and Denby went in for breakfast. Then he ate in the chrome and plastic and glass restaurant while the other two waited at the phone.

The early glare faded into the cold overcast of a slow-moving storm somewhere out of sight beyond the wall of mountains, and Wager wondered anxiously at the amount of business the telephone did. Hardly an hour went by when someone didn't use it, and they always seemed to spend at least twenty minutes gabbing and grinning and noting addresses.

"Maybe it's a bookie's phone," said Billington through the sliding window behind the truck's seat.

"Tourists," said Denby. "Used to be springtime was tourist season; now it's all the time. I've had seven sets of my wife's relatives visit us in the last six months. All with kids."

"Jesus. No wonder she likes to go to movies."

That was still a sore point with Denby. "Yeah. You think Francisco was pulling us through the grease?"

"If he was," said Wager, "I'll kill the son of a bitch."

A little after ten, an El Paso County sheriff's car pulled up and a figure wearing sunglasses stepped slowly from the cruiser to stare at their license plate before easing up to the truck. "You fellows having any trouble?"

Wager stepped down from the warmth of the cab and showed his identification. "We're waiting for a call from Denver telling us our suspect's on his way."

"Oh—sorry. The guy in the gas station was suspicious. Can our office help out?"

"We'll just wait here for the call."

"Well, if you want any help . . ."

166

"You'll hear us asking."

Near noon the phone rang. Sergeant Johnston's voice came through on a good connection this time: "I been calling the last half hour, but the goddam line was busy!"

"A lot of tourists have been using the phone."

"For Christ's said, you should have put up a sign saying it was out of order."

"I didn't think of it. What do you have?"

"Rafael and one Chicano male in his mid-twenties left the Rare Things at eleven-twenty-five. They drove to an apartment at 3422 Kalamath and picked up a 1972 Pontiac Le Mans, tan, license AF 1306. The second unit's with them now, driving a 1972 Impala, white over green, license BC 7508. They're on their way."

"Got it. We'll move to the rendezvous."

Denby leaned over his shoulder as he hung up. "That it?"

"Yeah." Wager flipped through the pages of his Alvarez journal. "They're driving Henry's Le Mans."

Billy looked at his watch. "Figure an hour?"

"Time for a quick lunch—unless you want me to cook up some canned chop suey."

"Tell you what: I'll buy you lunch if you promise not to cook."

After eating, they moved the truck to the wide pull-off that opened to a view of the distant Academy buildings glinting among dark pines on the foothills. The traffic on I-25 was light but steady, numbers of tractor-trailers blasting past and gearing down for the weigh station just up the road, cars whistling on the long decline into Colorado Springs from Monument Hill. At 1:35, a thin, terse voice came through the police frequency calling Wager's number. "We're on I-25 approaching the checkpoint. Acknowledge."

"Read you. Come up on two."

A few minutes later, the unmarked car passed and they pulled in behind it. "I didn't see any tan Le Mans," said Billy.

"Me either. I hope they didn't screw things up."

Billy keyed the transmit button: "We're behind you."

The same voice came in on a strong signal over channel 2: "We see you behind us. The suspects are three cars ahead, a 1974 Caddy El Dorado, black, Colorado license AN 2538."

"We heard they were driving a tan Pontiac Le Mans."

"They were. And then they switched again in the parking lot at Cinderella City. I didn't see them move any luggage; somebody else must have set it up this morning."

"A brand-new El Dorado! That son of a bitch likes to ride in style." Billy braced the glasses on his knee and peered through the windshield. "There it is—two men, license AN 2538. Man, I hope we can keep up with them."

Wager transmitted: "We have them now. Turn off whenever you want to."

"Roger. And good luck."

"Thanks."

The highway south from Colorado Springs skirted the edge of Fort Carson, and the only things breaking the monotony of rolling grassy hills were occasional tank hulls burned black from target practice. Then the road started its long tilts uphill and down across the prairie and the dry washes, and it was safe to let the Cadillac become a glittering black dot miles down the pavement. Wager pulled up close again as they neared Pueblo, but the black car stayed on the freeway arcing through and over the town, past the slag heaps and towering chimneys of the steel mills, and back onto the emptiness of the prairie. They made one stop at a roadside park, Wager slowing to ease the truck into a distant slot as the two men from the Cadillac went into the concrete bathroom.

"Man, I wish they'd hurry!" Denby danced up and down beside the truck and tried to stay out of the cold wind that flattened the stiff buffalo grass. Finally, the black car pulled onto the highway and Denby raced for the toilet.

"You think we'll have snow?" Billy studied the thick layer of high clouds that made the westering sun a pale circle.

"It sure feels like it."

"Maybe it'll slow the bastard down."

Harsh and cold, Greenhorn Mountain swung slowly past in the west, and at Walsenburg they picked up the Spanish Peaks looking close and sharp in the winter light. It began to snow just north of Trinidad, and by the time they gassed up and began the climb to Raton Pass, they had to turn on their lights in the grayness of snow and early dusk. Denby was driving now, hunching over the wheel and clenching his teeth as the truck edged awkwardly this way and that on the ice patches that began to glint on the highway.

"Can you see him up ahead?" asked Billy.

"Hell, I'm too busy to look!"

Wager, in the camper, climbed up to the small window at the front of the cabin. "I see some tail-lights—two sets—a mile or so up the road."

"Can you go a little faster?"

"Jesus, Billy, this thing's already sliding around."

They rode in tense silence as the wet snow began to make thick white streaks through the headlights.

"You think they'll drive all night?" Billy unwrapped a chocolate bar and passed it around.

"I think we'd better get closer to them."

"I'm doing what I can, Wager!"

"You want me to drive awhile?" asked Billy.

Denby stomped the gas pedal, making the rear of the truck twist sharply sideways. "No. I'll do it."

They crossed the pass and began to gain going downhill; Denby's hands clutched at the swaying wheel and his foot patted the brake pedal lightly.

"Is that them?" Billington pointed out faint red lights.

After a few minutes, Denby said, "No. That's a Ford."

The truck roared past the snow-crusted car, the other driver a pale, tense glimmer in the headlights' glow.

"Gabe, go up and see if you can spot them."

"The window's covered with snow. I can't see out."

"Goddam, goddam. All we have to do is lose the bastard. How fast are we going?"

Denby glanced quickly at the speedometer and then back to the highway, the sides of which were almost invisible under the snow. "Sixty . . . too goddam fast for this pile of crap."

"Keep on it. There's some more tail-lights."

Slowly they drew closer through the curtain of falling snow. Billy balanced the binoculars and squinted through them. "OK, OK—that's them. Slow down some."

The truck lurched as Denby yanked his foot off the gas and sighed deeply, his shoulders sagging with relief. "Son of a bitch! I don't want to do that again soon."

They followed the Cadillac's red lights along sweeping turns through the high valleys of northeast New Mexico, losing them for a frantic five minutes as they merged with other lights nearing Santa Fe.

"There—that gas station!" Wager pointed to the roadside where the empty Cadillac sat getting gas from a pump. "Pull in between the car and the building; I have an idea."

Denby eased the creaking vehicle across the snow-wet concrete between the sedan and the small office. "Trade places with Billy—take a minute or two to stretch."

"What are you going to do?"

"Fix it so we can see him." Wager opened the back door to peek through the door hinge. Both men were in the gas-station office talking to the attendant. Wager quickly hopped out and, swinging hard with a can of chow mein, split one of the tail-light lenses. He tugged out a ragged piece of red plastic and darted back to the truck. "OK, let's go."

Billy pulled the truck back into the traffic. "I think you just broke the law."

Wager studied the dent in the chow-mein label. "They don't make cans like they used to."

A few minutes later, they sighted the black car on the highway behind them, and they slowed to let it pass. The white glare of the naked bulb made it easy to spot the car and they dropped farther back in traffic.

"He's heading for Albuquerque."

"Probably stopped to find out the road conditions."

Early-evening traffic crowded the freeway between Santa Fe and Albuquerque; the snow was mixed with rain and beginning to freeze on the pavement. Occasionally they flashed past the winking blue light of a sand truck, but more often the slush froze in an icy sheet that kept Billy whistling half-tunes through his teeth as he twitched the wheel back and forth.

"Can you still see them?"

"No. Hey, upstairs!" He beat on the cab wall until Denby answered with a groggy "What?"

"Is that window clear yet?"

"Yeah, a corner of it."

"Use these—see if you can spot them." He passed the glasses through the sliding window into the cooler air of the drafty camper.

A minute or two later, Denby's head hung down from the

upper bunk. "They're about six cars up and getting in the right lane. I think they're looking for a place to stop."

"Keep your eye on them."

Billington changed lanes and slowed, and they waited word from Denby.

"Right—there they go into the Silver Spur Motel. It's up a block on the right."

"Speed up, Billy."

They flashed past the glare of the motel's wet neon, and Wager had a quick glimpse of one figure opening the office door while the other stood in the shelter of the apron and stretched his arms high.

"Take the next right and let's give them a few minutes."

Waiting fifteen, they returned down the highway and backed the truck into a side street two blocks from the motel. With the glasses, they could see the Caddy now parked in slot 10. Wager put the 1000-millimeter lens on the camera and shot a picture. Billy rummaged in the cooler and lifted out a Coors. "Who said they wanted a beer?"

Denby had the first watch, then Billy, and finally Wager. He was dusting the shells of a boiled egg out of his lap when he saw the Caddy's exhaust begin to smoke in the morning light. "Let's go."

"Wait a goddam minute!" Billy clanked pots and drawers in the camper. "I still got some dishwater to get rid of!"

"What the hell did you have to wash after boiling eggs?"

Denby climbed into the rider's seat and sleepily rubbed his nose with a handkerchief. "Jesus, it's cold. At least the snow's stopped. I wish I had some more coffee.

It gradually cleared and warmed as they went down New Mexico along the broad piñon-dotted valley between the San Andres Mountains and the Black Range. By one o'clock, when they arrived at Las Cruces, the cab windows were down and Denby was sneezing and cursing the dust. "Here"— Billy popped open another beer—"this'll help settle the dust."

When they reached El Paso, Denby was asleep in the heat of the camper. Billy said, "Let him sleep," and trained the glasses on the black Cadillac; its brake light flashed white in the traffic. "He's going to that motel."

"Right."

A half-hour later, the Cadillac, with Rafael driving and alone, was on its way again, down between the crowded signs nearing the border and into the line across the Cordova Street Bridge. Billy, now driving, nosed the truck up to the bored Mexican official waving cars past.

"Your destination, please?"

"Juárez."

"You're all United States citizens?" He peered at Wager.

"Right—we're down for a little, what do you call it, fiesta!"

"Ha, fiesta! *Bienvenido a México*—welcome to Mexico." His hand flapped them past.

"Hey, Gabe, you're right at home here!"

In time he might be, and it was an odd double-self feeling to think that outwardly he would be indistinguishable from the swarms of brown-faced people moving, standing, talking on the dirty sidewalks and curbs. But instead of feeling comfortably invisible, he felt even more isolated, because inwardly he would never be like them. Inwardly, he felt as alien and touristy as the patches of white faces—nosy, nervous, gap-mouthed with laughter—moving across the band of darker Mexican faces. It was not home, and though he had not really thought too much about it one way or the other, he was still a little surprised at the distance between him as a Hispano and these Mexicans. And he wondered if the younger Chicano kids, for all they said, felt any more at home down south. He felt like just another tourist wandering in strange streets, and the streets themselves had a total lack of dignity that almost made him sick: a tinsel carnival of color, loud recorded mariachis, hooting vendors, grimy kids tugging at tourists' sleeves, junky stores for junky customers, filth, hot smells, and—unending—the sense of humanity crowded too close to rub and spit and clutch without befouling each other. "Stick with Rafael—there he goes up there."

"I see him."

They closed up as much as the crowds of cars would let them, and followed the large black car as it turned in to a side street on which bars, shops, and lawyers' offices soon gave way to small hotels and finally to a fringe of tin and egg-crate shacks and crumbling adobe walls.

"Wow, what a smell!" Billy said. "Hey, Denby, did you

172

brush your teeth this morning?''

His muffled voice answered from the hot cab: "I brush my teeth every morning!''

"Then it must be you, Gabe. Your Mexican's starting to ooze out.''

"You smell your upper lip.''

The truck lurched off the rough pavement into a cloud of dust raised by the car ahead. Through the clatter and squeal of gear in the back, they heard Denby sneeze a dozen times.

"He's turning right.''

The slum section suddenly gave way to larger houses, with more space between them and surrounded by thick stone walls topped by broken bottles stuck in concrete. As the road climbed a small rise and cars grew even scarcer in the clinging dust, Billy let the Cadillac move away. "I'm pretty sure I remember where he's headed. We're getting near Valdez's place.'' He gazed intently at the brightly trimmed houses rising over the peeling street walls. "Yeah, I remember for sure now. It should be up another turn and then off to the left. We'll be able to see the house soon.''

Reaching the turn, Billy pointed to the boxy house rising yellow-white in the late-afternoon glare. Like the others, it had iron grilles over the first-floor windows and trays of bright flowers along the second floor. The flowers and heat and glare made it hard to realize it was late October. Billy drove past the street, then swung the truck around in a rutted alley between two blank walls. They eased back down the slope until they could see the black car shimmering in the silent whiteness of the dirt road. Wager shot a few pictures with the 300-millimeter lens and they waited.

At 5:17, Rafael came out; Billy and Wager ducked out of sight behind the dash while Denby, muffling sneezes and cursing the heat trapped by the baking tin roof of the camper, took pictures through the front window and told them what was happening.

"He's turning around and waiting. Here comes another car out of the driveway. A 1972 Buick Special, metallic blue, Mexican plates. A man's driving, accompanied by a woman passenger. Stay low, here they come.''

Wager heard the Caddy's tires crunch through the dirt, followed by the Buick.

"It's Valdez," he told Billy. "Valdez probably has the dope. He'll cross it in his car and then transfer it to Rafael."

"You want to stay with them?"

"Give them plenty of room."

The two cars went directly back to the Cordova Street Bridge Port of Entry. Denby could see over the line of cars between them as they queued up to cross. The Cadillac was held up for a quick search of the trunk and a look at Rafael's identification; the Buick, two or three cars back, was greeted with a smile and a quick wave.

"Christ, they didn't even open the trunk!"

"That's his reward for being a snitch—all the heroin he can carry."

The customs inspector leaned to their window. "You're all American citizens?" He gazed at Wager. "You got identification, sir?"

The three showed their drivers' licenses.

"Anything to declare?"

"Nothing."

"Would you open up the back, please?"

"Hell," whispered Denby through the cab window, "let's show him our law-enforcement ID before we lose them."

"Sit tight. I can still see the Buick. And we better not take a chance on a leak—you going to tell him we're following his buddy that he just waved past?"

A few clumps and bumps in the camper; then the agent motioned them on.

"The Buick turned right four blocks down."

"OK." Billy swerved around a slow line of cars, ignoring the startled anger of horns. "They've gone to the motel."

The two cars were in the motel's parking lot. Rafael and his rider came out of the line of rooms and led the Buick back downtown. They followed the white flash of the broken tail-light through the early-evening traffic to the Continental Bus Lines depot. There the cars pulled to the curb, and the woman got out of Valdez's car and opened the trunk. Rafael carefully stayed out of sight of the package that his rider lifted out of the Buick's trunk. The rider and the dope disappeared into the bus station. Valdez and the woman pulled away, and Rafael, after waiting a moment or two, headed back to his motel. The big meet was over.

174

13

They made the call to Denver to alert surveillance at the bus depot, then took turns driving and dozing in swaying restlessness; at nine Sunday morning, the camper pulled into the small asphalt lot beside OCD headquarters. The boxy building had an unchanged look that made Wager almost doubt the reality of the last few days' kaleidoscope of alien scenery. It felt as if they had been gone for a long time, but it felt, too, that they had never left. Nothing seemed to have missed them.

Denby and Billington said weary good-byes in the empty lot, and Wager, his arms loaded with camera equipment, let himself into the building. As he climbed the familiar, musty, dark stairs, he felt the routine of the headquarters wrap around him and heard what he had been unconsciously waiting for: thin radio music from the distant duty room. No one answered his call to the photo lab, and the DPD desk confirmed it: "Ain't nobody there now, Detective Wager. They'll be open eight o'clock Monday." He wondered a few minutes about calling Sergeant Johnston this early on Sunday, then figured what the hell, Johnston was a cop, too.

"Ed? This is Gabe. We just got back."

Johnston spoke with a mouth full of breakfast: "What about Rafael?"

"He'll probably be getting in sometime tomorrow. Any word from the bus station?"

"Not yet. I thought you might be them."

"I'm going home to clean up. Call me there when something breaks."

He half expected the call to come while he was in the shower, and he set the phone on the back of the toilet just in case. But it didn't. He toted it into the kitchen and made an omelette—onions, chives, hot peppers, and soy sauce—then carried it back to the living room and thumbed through the Sunday papers. No call. By four in the afternoon, after a restless doze in which he kept hearing the telephone jangle him awake, he finally called back. "What happened, Ed—that bus should be in by now."

"It got in. But the runner wasn't on it."

"What the hell happened?"

"The driver said a man answering the description you gave us and carrying a brown package got off in Castle Rock. We guess someone met him there and brought him the rest of the way in."

"That's a bite in the ass."

"Well, we're all set up on Rafael. We got primary and backup people at every known location."

"Fine. That's better than the nothing we've got now." He hung up and dialed Francisco's number: no answer. He tried the number every fifteen minutes until finally, at eight, a guarded voice said, "Hello?"

"This is Wager. The El Paso deal went through and Rafael's on his way back. He should be in tomorrow. You let me know when that cut is."

"Hey, man, I don't always know!"

"You better know this time. I mean it."

"You said you owe me!"

"Without Rafael there isn't a damn thing to owe." He hung up and stalked through the apartment, silently cursing himself for not putting a man on the bus with the runner, cursing Alvarez for outthinking him, cursing Denby because he was good to curse.

But the waiting was different this time. Before, they hadn't been certain that something was really going to happen; this time, they knew the other shoe would drop eventually. Rafael had too much cash tied up in the dope to let it sit forever; he had customers who would start looking somewhere else if he didn't provide. Business was business, and time was overhead. Yet it still took eight days before Wager got his call.

"It's for you." Suzy pressed his extension number, and Wager, not really expecting it, said, "Detective Wager."

"The cut's set for this afternoon. I don't know where it is and I ain't about to ask."

"What time?" His voice made Denby look up from the letter he was writing.

"About three." The line clicked dead.

"Got something?"

"It's this afternoon—call Billy, tell him to haul his butt down here." Wager strode to Sergeant Johnston's office. "The tip just came in—it's this afternoon."

"Right." Johnston began dialing. "Let the Inspector know."

Sonnenberg, the inevitable cigar smoldering in his ashtray, nodded. "Everything ready? Need anything?"

"We've been ready. Rafael's at the Rare Things and I'm going out there now."

Denby was on the telephone and wagged his hand at Wager. "Yeah? OK . . . OK, got it. That was Otero. He says the phone at the Rare Things is getting hot—they're setting up locations for drops starting tomorrow."

In his mind, Wager could almost hear Rafael's voice telling his ounce man where the initial location would be, then calling at the last minute and changing the location to throw off any tails. "That ties it. Let's go."

They came toward the store from different directions and stopped in a wide circle on distant streets. Billy was waiting when Wager checked into the net.

"We're all set—a mouse couldn't get through."

"It's a snake we're after."

At 2:42, unit 5 broke silence: "Suspect is leaving the Rare Things in a red-over-black '73 Firebird, Colorado plates AS 3101. Heading west on Thirty-eighth. All units acknowledge."

Wager waited his turn and answered, "Unit three. I'm parallel on Forty-first."

"Suspect turning north on Federal. Unit three pick him up."

That was Wager. He slowed until he saw the Firebird cross in front of him, then turned in behind. "Got him. Thirty-five miles an hour heading north." Rafael crossed I-70, jamming the grid of chase cars onto the single overpass, and then swung sharply east on the frontage road. "East on Forty-eighth, forty-five miles an hour. Somebody get over to the Pecos interchange."

Billy's voice shot in: "Unit one, will do." Three minutes passed and his disgusted voice came up again: "Crap, he just passed me heading south on Pecos. Double back quick."

Wager stayed with the speeding Firebird until suddenly it swerved to the curb and slowed to a crawl, an arm in the window waving cars past. "Unit three. I think he spotted me; he stopped in the forty-four-hundred block." He sped past the Firebird and then slowed to work his way into a distant side street. "He's still there. He's waving cars past him. I'm ahead of him now on Pecos."

"Unit two," said Denby. "I see him now. Gabe, take the left parallel; I'm behind him now."

"Roger."

The grid of chase cars fanned out again. Alvarez swung close to the Rare Things and began cutting through alleys, zigzagging across northwest Denver and popping up into the zones of the grid.

"He's starting to circle the block of Thirty-second and Eaton."

Circling the block, Rafael varied his speed to come up behind anyone tailing him; the pursuit cars pulled away and waited at the edge of vision. Wager could see, two blocks away, the Firebird swing time after time around the single block.

"I'm getting dizzy watching him."

"There he goes, Billy. He's on your parallel."

"Roger."

Now he began driving directly south and the grid shifted to cover Billy's flanks. Once again the Firebird pulled over and waved traffic past. Denby moved in behind and Billy swung around the block to take Denby's parallel.

"He's off again. West on Sixth."

"We're behind you." Another limited-access highway; Billy, Wager, and the three other units fell into a loose column spread over a couple of miles.

"He's pulling over again. He sure likes that trick."

Unit 6, last in line, slowed while the other pursuit units passed the suspect and spread out on the Wadsworth interchange to wait.

"Unit six. Suspect is moving now. West at thirty-five miles an hour. I'm turning off at Wadsworth."

178

"Roger. We'll come down behind him."

The Firebird moved slowly down the right lane of the highway, the rest of the traffic speeding past him.

"Unit two," said Denby. "I'm passing him. I'll wait at the Kipling interchange."

A few minutes later, the suspect turned at Kipling. "I got him, I see him." Denby's voice was excited. "He's going north at forty miles an hour."

"Stay with him, Denby." Here the side streets curved and dead-ended; the only pursuit was directly behind. Wager cautioned the pursuit cars to stretch out the column.

"He's turning in to the Royal Lodge Apartments, 4710 Kipling. I'll double back on him."

"Right." Wager read quickly through the notebook and found the address: Henry's drop, the apartments with that nice helmet and shield in antique plastic. He and the other cars quickly spread in a semicircle around the only exit from the apartments.

"He's parking," said unit 4. "He's going into the second building. You want to move in now?"

"Wait. It could be a decoy." It wouldn't be the first time a suspect stopped at an address to trigger a premature arrest. They'd go storming in with a no-knock, and there Rafael would sit grinning and drinking a beer and not a gram of dope on the premises.

They waited eight long, tense minutes. "He's coming out slow," said unit 4. "He's carrying what looks like a bundle of clothes. Maybe it's the stash." And maybe it was a bundle of clothes. "He's just sitting in the car, doing nothing."

"Let him sit," said Wager.

Exactly five minutes later, Rafael started his car and turned up onto nearby I-70 and headed straight east toward town. Now he moved with the traffic, directly to I-25 and south for seven and a half miles to the Downing interchange. He turned right on Downing to Evans and then west again, making no attempt at evasion. At 2110 Oneida, he parked in the driveway of a small fieldstone house. Wager, looking twice through his notebook, did not recognize the address. But he did recognize the Mach-1 that pulled up in half an hour. He gave them another twenty minutes, then keyed the mike: "All right, this looks like the place. Units five and six, stay mounted. The rest of you people, park around the corner on Pontiac. I'll meet you there."

There were five officers. Wager spread them around the small house, setting Denby to cover the back door. Then he and Billy walked carefully up the tilting slabs of the old concrete walk and across the groaning porch boards. The screen was latched and the front door closed. Wager carefully slit the screen, pressing its rusty sag against the door to silence the twanging cut. He lifted the hook and looked at Billy.

Billy took a deep breath and nodded.

Slamming his shoulder against the cracking panels of the old door, Wager flung it open with a spray of screws from the lock and leaped inside. Billy kneeled low to cover him, aiming into the dark of the curtained and empty front room. A startled "What the fuck!" came from the kitchen and Wager had a glimpse of a wide-eyed face peering around the doorframe just before the door slammed shut.

"Police raid," shouted Wager. "You're under arrest!" Billy sprinted past him and crashed into the kitchen door, splitting it off its hinges as someone howled from the kitchen, "The pigs—the fucking pigs!"

"Hold it, you son of a bitch!" Billy, kneeling beside the shattered door, cocked the pistol hammer and leveled it with both hands braced on his knee. Spread over the kitchen table were small mounds of light and dark brown powder, cut into varying grades and waiting to be measured in the chemist's scales. "Jesus! Look at all that shit!"

Wager, glancing beyond the table full of low mounds, spotted a second figure easing toward the window. He recognized the young face he had glimpsed at the Clarkson Street drop, Labelle's supplier. "Down on your ugly face, goddam you, or I'll blow you apart! Spread—spread, you son of a bitch!" He jabbed the muzzle of his pistol hard under the man's ear and mashed his face against the worn linoleum. Savagely twisting the stiff arms up, he squeezed one handcuff tight around a wrist and looped the chain under the man's wide leather belt before locking the other cuff tightly. Billy, kneeling on his suspect's kidneys, waved his pistol toward the back door where the blurred figure of Rafael jumped from the shadows and across the small porch. Rafael reached for

180

the door handle, missed, and ripped through the screen and frame, stumbling into the back yard and then sprinting for the alley.

"Get the bastard—there he goes—get him!"

Denby rose from behind a low shrub and lunged at the figure, grabbing his coat and yanking it off as Rafael shrugged out of it and kept running. Wager started left around the tilting box of an old garage while Denby, swearing, angled right. Wager rounded the frayed wood of the building in time to see Denby dive over a garbage barrel and snag Rafael's foot, tumbling him hard on the tarred alley. There was a blur of arms and fists, then Wager laid his pistol barrel over Rafael's head and the only sound was Denby's breathless grunting, "Goddam, goddam, goddam, I broke my goddam arm."

The day after the arrest, Inspector Sonnenberg called Wager in: "I want you and me and Cole to go over everything you've got on these people."

Cole was one of the most experienced men on the District Attorney's staff. "You think something's wrong with the evidence?"

"I want to make damn sure it isn't. You know who this Rafael's got for a lawyer?" He waited until Wager shook his head. "F. Paul Chadwick."

"That guy from San Francisco?"

"That's the one."

Wager blinked. "I guess they can afford the best money can buy."

"Cole will handle the case. You and Denby will give him all the help he needs, understand? Nothing else until this case is over."

"Yes, sir."

"How's Denby's arm?"

"He hurts, but the doctor says he'll be able to come back tomorrow."

"Fine. Did he see the papers?"

A headline cited Denby's role in the biggest drug bust in Denver history; a three-column photograph showed a pained Denby, one arm dangling oddly, the other hand on Rafael's shoulder, stepping through the doorway of the police building. "Yes, sir. I brought him a copy but he already had a couple of his own."

"A reporter wants to do a story on the bust—and it couldn't come at a better time: the Joint Budget Committee's hearing our request next week. I'm going to have Denby sit with me when we present our request. You tell him that."

"Yes, sir."

"Now let's help the DA build this case."

Preliminary hearings are the worst part; Wager always had the feeling at these sessions—which could spread out over so many weeks and drag through endless formalities of procedure—that it wasn't the criminal but the police who were on trial. This feeling was reinforced as the case became the DA's and he sat waiting to give evidence, to explain, to justify police action at this or that point, to serve as a tool for the presecutor's use in building the paper case that was far more important than he or Billy or Denby or even Rafael, sitting wooden-faced behind the defense table.

In the gallery, strangely crowded with reporters and Alvarezes of all connections, sat Henry. He leaned forward the whole time, listening, his dark eyes moving in steady rhythm from face to face as Cole outlined the stages of the investigation. Except for the suit, whose cut and color told as many people as possible how expensive it was, Henry looked like a successful businessman; the gray streaks over his temples made him look distinguished—fitting his new role as head of the family. But he was too busy to pose; Henry was busy learning from Rafael's bust. He would lead the second generation of rats, Wager knew; would be smarter than the first, and harder to kill. Henry was furthering his education.

The plea was guilty; sentencing set for two weeks hence. Wager turned in his front-row seat and peered past the suddenly restless heads into young Anthony's hot eyes and smiled. For a long second, Anthony stared back in tense rage; then the handsome, clean-shaven face nodded once, accepting the challenge, and he and Uncle Henry joined the murmuring crowd as it left. A couple of new assistant DAs slapped Cole's shoulders and stared curiously at the tall figure of Chadwick; beyond the crowd of lawyers and reporters swirling around the San Franciscan, Rafael was hustled, almost invisible, out the side door of the courtroom.

Billy, standing beside Wager, sighed deeply. "We finally got one! Hey, what's this I hear about Denby?"

Wager nodded. "It's true." Denby had a job offer from Los Angeles.

"Is he going?"

"Yeah. His wife wants him to have regular hours. And he says there's less allergy problems there."

"Jesus. There ain't no justice."

GREAT READING FROM BERKLEY

ASSASSIN   (03094-6—$1.50)
    by Robert Kearney

FUNERAL IN BERLIN   (03251-5—$1.50)
    by Len Deighton

THE JOSEPH FILE   (03118-7—$1.50)
    by Alfred Harris

McIVOR'S SECRET   (03275-2—$1.50)
    by Lee Grimes

OPERATION NIGHTFALL   (03087-3—$1.75)
    by John Miles & Tom Morris

THE STRASBOURG LEGACY   (03263-9—$1.50)
    by William Craig

THE ULLMAN CODE   (03137-3—$1.75)
    by Robert Bernhard

WESTMINSTER ONE   (03112-8—$1.75)
    by Ted Willis

Send for a *free* list of all our books in print

These books are available at your local bookstore, or send
price indicated plus 30¢ per copy to cover mailing costs to
Berkley Publishing Corporation
390 Murray Hill Parkway
East Rutherford, New Jersey 07073